AN
ANGEL CAME
DOWN

or

THE
ANGEL OF
ALL CANNINGS

A Mystical Thriller

by

J.P. WARNER

Is there something dark at the heart of the Pewsey Vale?

Published by Tiddlywink Books

First published in Great Britain in 2006 by Tiddlywink Books.

1   2006

ISBN 0-9553730-0-X (10 digit)
ISBN 978-0-9553730-0-8 (13 digit)

To order further copies or to contact the author:
Tiddlywink Books
PO Box 3115, Devizes, SN10 9AQ, UK
Email: anangelcamedown@hotmail.co.uk
Tel.: 07804 507970

Printed and bound in Great Britain by Antony Rowe Ltd,
Chippenham, Wiltshire

This book is dedicated to the memory of Frederick Henry Warner, a Royal Engineer, a Master Electrician and, most of all, an exceptional Father

With love and thanks to my wife, my mother, our families and our friends

CONTENTS

"But he's a boy, just a boy!" wailed the nurse.

"Get a hold of yourself, woman!" the Doctor snapped, his mind racing, his body prickling with cold sweat.

The young man who had just been brought in on a stretcher from the military ambulance was shaking wildly, his limbs flailing about, flecks of the thick, white foam around his mouth spattering on the prefabricated emergency room's floor.

"What the hell's wrong with him, Doc?" asked the ambulance driver. "I've never seen anything like this before."

"Just go!" said the Doctor firmly. "Actually, no. Wait. Hold his arms." The driver and the other member of the ambulance crew did as they were told. "Right!" continued the Doctor, a large syringe in his hand, "Hold him steady!"

The young man, weakening with every convulsion of his body, his terrified eyes bulging red in their sockets darting this way and that, his sweat-sodden hair sticking to his forehead, never felt the needle snap in his arm. With one final leap, as if hit with a mighty electric shock, his body lurched up off the table and thudded back, dead. The final sound to reach his ears was the nurse, quietly weeping.

The Doctor instinctively checked his watch to record the time of death and noticed his hand shaking uncontrollably as he did so. Dropping the syringe into a white enamelled metal dish, he walked slowly to the window and leant heavily on the metal sill, his breath fogging the glass as he fought to control his emotions.

He stared out across the bleak, snowy plain listening to the sound of the blood whistling in his ears, and then half-whispered, as if to himself: "Sometimes only death can bring you peace."

***

Hobbes Barracks
5th January 1963

Dear Jean,

It was smashing to be home with the family for Christmas but I didn't half miss you. I know you had to go to your Gran's with your Mum and Dad, so don't think I'm blaming you or anything. Anyway, I hope you had a nice time.

Bert kept ribbing me that you'd gone to the other end of the country to avoid me, but a clip round the ear sorted him out! He went and cried to Dad who told me I'm getting too big for my boots, and that National Service was supposed to stop us turning into young tearaways. He says it's a disgrace that I'll be one of the last to go. I told him I don't even remember the flaming

War, so I don't see what all the fuss is about. So he clipped <u>me</u> round the ear for talking back!

Anyway, love, I've got some good news! One of the other lads told me he's signed up for some tests to help find a cold cure or something. He says they send you away for the week to be prodded about by some eggheads in white coats and at the end of it you get a three day pass! I'm going to sign up first thing Monday morning.

Thanks for the Christmas present. I hope you liked the record I bought you. There's a scouse lad in the bunk two down from me says he knows one of the band's Mums and could get it autographed for you if you like. I shouldn't bother. It's not worth sending it all the way to Liverpool to get scrawled on by someone who no-one's ever going to remember.

Anyway, almost dinner time, so I'll sign off now. I'll let you know as soon as I get my leave sorted out so we can plan what we'll do. I'll write to my Mum to see if she'll talk to yours so we can all have a weekend at Bournemouth!

Say Happy New Year to your parents for me.

"Love me do!"

Your Jack xxx

PROLOGUE
1975

The Doctor looked out through the rain-flecked windscreen of his brown Austin Ambassador. A damp, misty Wednesday in March seemed only too fitting a backdrop for a visit to his wife's grave.

Enveloped in the mist of her clinical depression she had taken her own life two years before, finished off by the never-ending British winter. Marriage to a doctor had seemed such a good match for a young girl in the early 1960s but his incredibly long hours had almost entirely rid her of any social life and his unwillingness to discuss his work had left her feeling isolated and alone. Brought up in an era when no-one ever complained about their lot, all she could do was turn her suffering in on herself.

With a deep sigh, he turned off the engine, opened the door and left the cosseting warmth of his caramel-coloured velour driver's seat.

There was something perversely comforting about the All Cannings graveyard. Nestled behind a terrace of chocolate-box thatched cottages and the village school, it usually looked out across a wide working farmyard to

Salisbury Plain in the distance. Today, however, the doctor was glad the mist was obliterating the view.

As he crunched up the gravel path, the little church he knew so well loomed out of the fog. He automatically took the path to the right and was soon standing before his wife's grave. After a silent prayer, he unbuttoned the top of his overcoat, removed a perfect, pink rose from his buttonhole and crouched down to place it beside the headstone.

As he did so, the peace was suddenly shattered by a loud, deep moan and a scream. If the first had made him shudder, the second propelled him to his feet, looking in all directions. He had barely a moment to brace himself before someone came bowling out of the fog and almost knocked him flat on his back.

He looked down to see a pretty young blonde, clearly terrified, her arms locked around his torso and her head craning round to see whatever was pursuing her. Stiff as a board from the shock and the awkwardness of the situation (this was the closest any woman had been to him since his wife's passing), the doctor was wondering what to do next when the fearful noise began again.

Still shaking, the woman immediately felt him relax and, in search of a reason, looked up at him for the first time. A kind, but clearly world-weary face was smiling back at her.

"Frightening thing, fog," it said. Her eyes narrowed in incomprehension. "You can't see what's around you. It's very disorientating." Seeing he wasn't getting his point across, he tried again: "That dreadful noise. It's coming from the cow byre."

Her reaction to this news was not what he had expected. Rather than the sudden detachment, the stuttered apologies, the deep blush of embarrassment, she simply leant her head on his chest, and began to sob quietly. Instinctively, and to his own surprise, he began to stroke her hair and whisper words of comfort.

How long they stood like this, two strangers united in their respective loss, cocooned in a cotton wool world, unseen and unheeded, he couldn't say, but eventually he suggested a drink might do her good and they made their way to the Kings Arms, she still leaning on him for support.

Half an hour later, facing each other over a couple of empty brandy glasses and the remains of a perfect ploughman's lunch, he had learnt her name, her age (almost 15 years his junior) and, it seemed to him, her life's story. Her parents had died in a car crash when she was 20 leaving her a tidy sum. Her elder brother and his young wife had invited her to stay to get over the initial shock; she had never left.

When she asked him about himself, he trotted out his old cover story with a faint sense of self-disgust. How much longer would he have to lie to everyone in his life?

***

He had given her a lift home that first afternoon and, as the weeks went by, he had begun to pick her up to take her to the graveyard and then on to lunch or for a walk, often in complete silence, hand in hand, for hours.

And then, one bright, late summer's day, he arrived to find her waiting not with her usual posy of flowers but with a picnic basket, a blanket and a parasol. As they sat atop Knap Hill surveying the vast swathe of the Pewsey Vale below them, he removed his button hole, and handed it to her. They sat for a long time in silence, contemplating the significance of the gesture.

"I don't think I'll be going back to the graveyard again," he said eventually. "I want to concentrate on the future ... with you." Her smile reassured him. "Of course, I'll still bring you to see your parents," he added. A cloud of incomprehension passed quickly from her face.

"But it's not my parents in the graveyard," she said gently, "I go to see Jack."

***

Sitting, the calf muscle of his left leg twitching uncontrollably, the Doctor raised his gaze for the first time in the last five minutes to meet the cold, grey eyes of the Chief Medical Officer. It had all come out in a flood of words: He couldn't be involved in the programme any more. He'd given it almost twenty years of his life but now, especially after the loss of his wife, he needed to move on, to break away. He understood that the security of the programme was key but they knew he could be trusted. He just wanted to be set free. And as he spoke all he could think of was her, his part in her suffering and her Jack, lying dead, the needle broken in his arm. As she had told him the story of the first cruel loss of her life, he knew he had finally had all he could take of the programme and all it entailed.

A long moment passed as a trickle of cold sweat ran down the Doctor's left temple.

"You'll understand," the CMO said so abruptly that the Doctor jumped, "that we don't exactly advertise that it is possible to leave the programme under certain circumstances, one of which is emotional exhaustion." He paused. "But in this instance, I'm prepared to approve your release." He stood, smiling, and stretched out his right hand. "You've served us well. I'm sorry to see you go."

Almost floating to his feet in total relief, the Doctor grasped the CMO's outstretched hand like a dying man snatching at salvation, and shook it firmly, barely noticing the odd sensation like sweat pricking his palm. As he relaxed his hand to pull it away, however, the other man gripped harder still, his left hand now clamped vice-like on the Doctor's wrist.

It was then the Doctor felt the chilled tingling flowing up his right arm and across his chest, and vaguely sensed the presence of others entering the room behind him. His consciousness fading, his head rolled slowly sideways and then down, and his eyes focussed for the first time on the blood dripping onto the desk from the tightening grasp of their endless handshake.

As his legs gave way and the light faded from the room, he sank to the floor and finally found his peace.

***

Wiltshire Tribune February 5ᵗʰ 1976

Inquest Rules on Sudden Death

An inquest sitting in Salisbury last Thursday ruled that the sudden death of Geoffrey Grant, a private physician, was due to the sudden onset of septicaemia. A keen cultivator of rare roses, 45-year-old Dr Grant was found dead in his garden last September.

The inquest heard that an examination of Dr Grant's swollen right hand had revealed scratches wholly consistent with those made by rose thorns. It was concluded that, left untreated, these infected wounds had led to the rapid onset of blood poisoning and the doctor's death.

Verdict: Death by misadventure.

CHAPTER 1
TOTALLY WEIRD

"Don't wanna go!" wailed J, as Em carried him through the front door.

"Yeah, I know, J," Em sighed, "neither do I but we have to. Dad can't breathe in the city. It's making him ill".

She looked around to make sure Mum hadn't heard. She'd promised not to mention Dad's breathing problems to J, but with all that was going on she'd forgotten. She turned to Joe. "Take J for a minute, would you? He's doing my head in."

It had been a horrible day and no way to say goodbye to a house they loved. A crying toddler to look after while Mum and Dad ran around trying to keep one step ahead of the removals men, who had descended at 6 a.m. like a cloud of locusts. They were now busy stripping the house of everything that marked it out as being a home, turning it back into just an empty shell.

"I told you we should've gone to stay at Gran's," grumbled Joe, who was distracting J with PB, his favourite polar bear toy. "This just sucks. It's like being burgled while you're still at home." Em knew what he meant.

Why was it that just when they were getting old enough to enjoy all the city had to offer, they had to move to some backwater in the middle of nowhere? It was going to be totally weird.

***

The car journey was unusually quiet. Dad drove in silence with the odd road direction from Mum, who was map reading. Joe and Em listened to their MP3 players and looked glumly out of opposite windows at first the motorway traffic and then the green-hedged country lanes. Even J, sandwiched between them in his baby seat, sensed something sad was happening and lazily chewed on PB's ear.

For the first time in what seemed like weeks, Em had a chance to just sit and think.

In some ways she was glad to be leaving the city. Her break-up with Mike had been really upsetting and he'd gone out of his way to be hurtful and to embarrass her in front of her mates. Joe had offered to "sort him out" but she didn't want to look as if she couldn't fight her own battles.

What had she ever seen in him? Mum was probably right (sickening as it was to admit it); love and sex are different things. And that was what ended it, really.

She couldn't work out why Mike would try to pressure her into sex before she was ready. What was it Dad had called him? "One big raging hormone"?

Mike also knew what she thought of her classmates who had had "accidents" and then dropped out to have children and spent their days roaming the shopping malls with their bored looking babies. It seemed that as soon as they'd given birth they were handed a shell suit, a baseball cap, a spotty boyfriend and an endless supply of fags. What sort of a life was that? She wasn't any different to anyone else, she wanted sex too, but not at any price and certainly not at *that* one.

***

Finally they drove into a courtyard surrounded by what looked like agricultural buildings. Silently they all got out of the car. Dad was the first to speak.

"I thought the letting agent said it was a barn conversion?"

"Well, it's a converted stable block," conceded Mum, "but it's lovely inside, I promise!" She slipped her arm through his and led him to the front door. Em and Joe stood looking around while J toddled off to investigate a flowerbed beside a patch of lawn.

"Nice flowers," said Joe. It was the first thing he'd said in three hours.

"What?" snapped Em, tetchily.

"Yeah, that was a bit lame. I was just trying to cheer you up," mumbled Joe, embarrassed.

"Oh! Right, sorry," said Em, looking around for a way to change the subject and pointing to a large house visible through the trees. "So what do you reckon that is, then?".

"That's 'The Bastion'," called Mum from the front doorstep, having now found the right key for the lock. "An old friend of your Grandpa's lives there. General Harris. He's a bit old-fashioned but a real sweetie."

"No-one who's spent their entire career trying to kill people could possibly be described as 'sweet'," mumbled Dad, provoking one of Mum's disapproving not-in-front-of-the-children shushes.

"Look," said Mum, "the removals van will be here in a minute so why don't you all have a quick loo break or whatever and then go for a walk around the village for about an hour? Then we can have tea and sort all our bedrooms out for tonight."

***

As her husband and the children wandered off, Anna was happy to get some time alone in the house before the removals commandos burst in, launching into their cardboard-boxed mayhem.

Coming home was never easy. She'd been dying to come back to her parents' house after university but somehow it wasn't the same home she remembered when she was growing up. She'd been terribly homesick when she'd travelled alone round the world (making her a real pain when watching any holiday programme: "Oh, I've been there!") and then painfully aware of why she'd gone travelling the moment she'd got back. And now, she was returning to the stamping ground of her youth.

Funny to think that it was her need to express herself, "to breathe" as she used to say, that had made her move away to the city and her husband's physical need to breathe that had brought her back. Ironic for him that as a former motoring writer who had also worked for a number of oil companies, he was now escaping from the city and the traffic fumes that were making his asthma life-threatening.

But this new house was good, she felt that. It was solid, it was warm and it had wonderful views of the

13

hills above the village. The highest points in Wiltshire the letting agent said. And that was exactly what they needed now: a solid foundation and a positive outlook.

***

The village turned out to be bigger than Em and Joe expected. Unwilling as they were to come here and hoping against hope that they'd never have to, they'd closed their minds to finding out anything about the place. It was just "the middle of nowhere, where nothing ever happens."

In fact, the main street was the best part of a mile long with many side lanes and footpaths. At the southern end of it was an enormous playing field in front of an old church with a clock tower that looked as if it had been tacked on as an afterthought.

As they approached, the clock chimed with a thin metallic "ding".

"Clock!" squealed J with delight, letting go of Em's hand and running across the grass towards it.

"Well that's him settled," laughed Dad. "What about you two?"

"Just where exactly are we Dad?" moped Joe.

"Ahem," coughed Dad, preparing to launch into his best tour guide monotone. "All Cannings, Wiltshire. Six-hundred-and-fifty inhabitants and some 200 dwellings, a school, a community-run shop and (thank God) a pub, in the heart of the sleepy Vale of Pewsey. To the north is the Kennet and Avon Canal and a lot of big hills, the highest points in the county. To the south, Salisbury Plain, the army's favourite playground, oh, and not forgetting your grandparents' house."

14

"Is that it?" said Joe, unimpressed.

"No. Five miles that way," Dad stuck out an arm "is the market town of Devizes and eight miles that way," he stuck out his other arm "is Marlborough with its famous school and more posh, young totty than you can shake a stick at."

"Urgh, Dad!" cringed Em.

"Sorry," conceded Dad, raising his hands in mock surrender, "that last bit was for Joe. Mind you," he nudged Em's arm "they do have lots of boys there too!"

"Could we *please* change the subject?" grimaced Em as Dad chuckled. "What exactly is there for us to do around here?"

"Well, you can go for a walk, ride a bike, ride a horse, ride a motorbike – no, scratch that one – paraglide off the big hills – actually, no, scratch that too. Hmm! Not a lot then, really!" Still laughing, Dad looked into the unamused faces of his eldest off-spring. "And your mother said how happy you'd be when I was back to my old self again. OK, look, I know it looks a bit grim right now but give it a go and ..."

"Whoosh! Whoosh! Whoosh!" Three fighter jets suddenly flashed overhead and shot off towards Salisbury Plain.

"What the ...?" shouted Joe.

"Welcome to the sleepy Vale of Pewsey!" shouted back Em, as sarcastically as she could.

CHAPTER 2
LITTLE GREEN MEN

The first few days at the new house were spent
unpacking, arranging and rearranging furniture and
generally settling in. Keeping a close eye on his
children's mood, Dad decided he needed to cheer the
twins up and took them and J off to explore Devizes.

Their first port of call was the library where J lost no
time cornering the huge soft toy crocodile, snake,
flamingo and bees in the children's section. Dad and the
twins took it in turns to keep an eye on him while the
others looked for something to occupy the large amounts
of spare time they were convinced they were going to
have.

"I think you should read *this*," Dad said to Joe,
picking out a slim paperback from one of the shelves. "It
was one of my favourites at your age. I think Em would
like it too."

"*War of the Worlds*?" read Joe, doubtfully. "I thought
you didn't like us reading violent stuff."

"This is different. It's science fiction, and I don't
remember it being that violent, though I suppose it must
be. A lot of stuff gets obliterated but I won't spoil it for

16

you. Anyway, it might give you some background for what we're doing tomorrow night."

"What? Obliterating stuff?" said Joe, hopefully.

"My lips are sealed," Dad smiled.

***

Reading it that afternoon, Joe was more than surprised to find that this book, written over a hundred years earlier, was actually pretty good. Aliens from Mars landing on Earth and massacring people with death rays. If only they handed this stuff out at school instead of Shakespeare, he thought, he might be bothered to pay attention once in a while.

Dad, it turned out, had been talking to Grandpa. As the twins sank down into their grandparents' welcoming sofa that evening after one of Grandma's exquisite meals (even better tonight as she was celebrating their arrival), Grandpa popped his head around the door and silently beckoned Em and Joe to follow him.

Out in the garden, a silhouetted figure was hunched over with its back to them. It was Great Aunt Mary, Grandpa's sister, who lived with Grandma and Grandpa. She had never married, though Mum had hinted that she had had quite a few "romances", as she called them, in her day.

Hearing them approach, she stepped aside to reveal a long, white telescope, mounted on an old wooden tripod, pointing heavenwards.

"Here's something you can't do in the city with all that light pollution," she said triumphantly. "Have a look through this!" Em went first, while Joe looked up in the direction the telescope was pointing.

"Are you looking at the Moon?" he asked.

"Close," replied Grandpa. "Go left a bit and you'll see what looks like a bright star. In fact, it's a planet, the closest one to earth; it's Mars."

"But why's it shining like that?" asked Em, letting Joe have a turn.

"It's just the Sun's light shining off it," said Grandpa "in the same way its light reflects off the Moon."

"Not just that," added Aunt Mary. "It's that bright because it's the nearest to Earth it's been for a very long time indeed."

"Hang on!" said Joe excitedly. "That's just like in the book Dad got me to read! The Martians wait for the orbits to bring the two planets together and then launch their rockets at the Earth."

"Oh, really?" laughed Grandpa. "Well I can't promise you little green men but I am taking you to the Science Museum tomorrow night to see it in detail as it reaches its closest point to us, its opposition."

"Are we going back to London?" Em asked with a sudden rush of enthusiasm.

"Oh, no dear, I'm sorry," said Grandpa, sensing her immediate disappointment. "We have a Science Museum of our own just up the road here near Swindon. It houses all the things they can't display in London – cars, planes, satellites and the like – and they're having a special event to allow people to see live satellite downlinks from the world's largest telescopes. It'll be great!"

"Yeah, I'm sure it will. Thanks Grandpa!" said Joe, trying to sound as positive as possible to cover Em's evident disappointment. It was clear his grandparents and Aunt Mary had gone to a lot of effort to welcome them and he didn't want to hurt their feelings.

***

The following evening was more eventful than expected. Dad stayed at home to babysit J and Mum drove the twins to pick up Grandpa and Aunt Mary before heading to the museum.

Presentations were made by "representatives of the British space industry" (prompting Grandpa to grunt that their existence was news to him) and, more importantly, there were a lot of young people there. This was a surprise to the twins, who had always believed that the city was for young people and the country was a place where old people went to die.

Em had begun to sense that something about Joe had been changing lately and now, away from all the background noise of the recent major upheaval in their lives, she could instantly see what it was: he was starting to show a real interest in girls.

"See anything you like?" Em suddenly asked him, causing his head to snap back from where he had been looking and turn a subtle shade of beetroot.

"I meant the exhibits," Em teased "but now you come to mention it …"

"I don't know what you're talking about," he argued weakly "I was looking at … at that plane."

"And the cute red-head standing in front of it's a minor detail, I suppose," smiled Em. "Look, why don't you just go over and say hello?" she added kindly.

"'Hello'?" said Joe flatly "Is that it? The full benefit of your superior dating experience? Perhaps I could try: 'Do you come here often?' as well!"

"What you say's not that important, you know," encouraged Em. "Not if she likes the look of you ..."

"And if she doesn't?"

"Well, then we'll all chip in and get her a guide dog. Go on! She's on her own now and she's looking this way." Reluctantly, and with a little shove from Em, Joe shuffled across the room to his destiny.

"That was nice," said Mum, coming over to Em's side. "I like it when you support each other."

"Come on," said Em, taking Mum's arm "let's not stand here staring. He's nervous enough as it is. Where's Grandpa got to?"

They turned to see him standing talking to Aunt Mary but looking straight past her.

"I think he's admiring the plane too!" giggled Em.

"Your Gran's right, you know," sighed Mum "they never grow up."

***

As the days went on the Vale's reputation for sleepiness took a steady battering. Fighter jets, transport planes, helicopters, military and private, and even microlites like enormous buzzing mosquitoes provided a unique sound track, often to the booming beat of artillery practice on the Plain. Even the nights were a struggle, with a low hum, that seemed to reverberate through the entire house, turning out to be a grain drier in the farm at the other end of the village.

The new surroundings affected J most of all, meaning the mornings were beginning more often than not before dawn. Given the tough time Mum had had after the birth of her third child, the whole family had got into the habit of rising together, whatever their alarm clocks said, in a show of solidarity.

One semi-comatose breakfast time, after a pitch black stormy night of howling wind and lashing rain, Dad looked up blearily from his porridge as the first glow of sunrise lit the horizon.

"Whoever said the countryside was peaceful was talking total b …"

"Darling!" scolded Mum

"… balderdash, dear. Balderdash."

"That's the problem with you townies," teased Mum, "You don't understand this is a working landscape not a museum exhibit."

"Can you let us know whether you'll be buying us all Hunter wellies and Barbour jackets now or are you waiting for Christmas?" hit back Dad.

"What *are* you two going on about?" interrupted Em, annoyed; the lack of sleep was starting to take its toll. Her parents looked at each other and theatrically raised their eyebrows.

"Get down!" commanded J from his high-chair. Em, who was already standing up, on her way to make more toast, lifted him out and he ran to stand on his favourite chair overlooking the neighbouring farmyard. He began to shout out excitedly what he could see:

"Blue tractor. Green tractor. Yellow digger. Angel."

"So what are we going to do today?" asked Mum in her best cheery voice.

"Blue tractor. Green tractor. Yellow digger. Angel."

"I'll think I'll wait for it to start first, thanks," yawned Joe, reaching for the teapot for a much-needed refill.

"Blue tractor. Green tractor. Yellow digger. Angel."

"Yes," said Dad picking up on Mum's cue, "didn't I promise you all a trip to the seaside?"

"No," grunted Joe.

"Blue tractor. Green tractor. Yellow digger. Angel."

"Well, I am now, grumpy. What do you think?" There was a pause.

"To be honest," said Joe "my head hurts and all I'm thinking is 'what angel is he on about?'"

As they each took in what Joe had just said, they all turned slowly towards J and followed his line of sight, first across into the farmyard, still shrouded in semi-darkness ("Blue tractor. Green tractor. Yellow digger.") and then up onto the hillside lit by the faint glow of the sunrise ("Angel!").

Spread across almost the entire gap between the farmhouse on the left of their view and the hay barn on their right was what looked like an enormous white paper cut-out and J was right, it did look like an angel. A triangle with a curved bottom, like a slice of cake, topped off with a circular head.

"Wicked! Nice one J!" said Joe. J beamed at his brother's approval.

"What is it?" asked Em, thrilled.

"Ah, I wondered how long it was going to be," yawned Dad dismissively, looking back at his breakfast. "Didn't we mention the alien visitors?"

"The what?" said Joe excitedly jumping up to join J at the window.

"The little green men that make the crop circles," he continued, not looking up. "They're like a pack of stray dogs going around leaving little messages all over the valley."

"Don't be so sarcastic," said Mum crossly from the other end of the table. She had always prided herself on keeping an open mind on all things, like being willing to try complementary therapies, no matter how much her husband might scoff and complain at the cost. "Lots of people think they're real, and not just the 'tree-hugging loonies' as you like to call them. This is mystical Wiltshire, you know. We have Stonehenge, Avebury, Silbury Hill …"

"Of course, there's only one blindingly obvious problem with your crop circle theory, Dad," cut in Em, who was now beside Joe and J at the window. "That hill's actually covered in grass."

It took a moment for this to sink in. Dad put his paper down and joined them at the window.

"So, who fancies a little walk then?" he said brightly.

***

It was barely light across the wide floor of the valley as Joe, Em and Dad crossed the canal bridge and took what seemed to be the most convenient footpath to the hillside. Though it was mid-summer, the night's storm had cleared to leave a clear sky and a distinct nip in the air.

As they trudged past hedgerows, they shocked a few sleeping birds into life, a precursor of the dawn chorus that they had now heard more times than they wished to remember.

As the gradient started to increase, pink and pale blue streaks of sunrise stretched across the sky. Suddenly, there was a sharp rasping sound, so loud and seemingly so close, they all jumped, and looked around startled.

"Up there!" said Em, pointing skywards.

At the top of one of the hills now towering above them was what looked like an enormous, floating light bulb, another rasp of flame shooting from its burner, revealing its true identity as a hot air balloon.

"Won't be long before we have the microlites and helicopters buzzing overhead, I suppose," sighed Dad. "Did I ever tell you I used to live in Exeter on the inner bypass, between a Post Office van depot and St David's railway station and never lost a wink of sleep?"

"Yeah Dad, you did, several times," slurred Joe, "but somehow it gets better every time you tell us." He ducked out of the way just in time to avoid a playful clip round the ear.

"Come on you two, stop mucking around. I want to see what it is," chivvied Em, striding ahead. Over a stile and up a steep slope they came through a small copse to make their final ascent to the site.

As they came closer to the Angel, which lay on a wide, flat, steeply sloping expanse of grassland, it became clear that there had been some sort of heavy impact at the centre of the roughly ten-metre wide "head", forming a crater a good four metres deep. This blow had thrown up the mass of white chalk debris that had fallen down the slope creating the 30-metre long triangular body.

The three had just completed a circuit of the Angel when the fledgling dawn chorus gave way to the faint "wacka-wacka" of helicopter blades that steadily grew louder and louder until it filled the air.

"What did I tell you?" smiled Dad but as he looked up his face changed and Em and Joe soon felt the strong downdraught. There was more than one helicopter and they were coming in to land.

Within seconds, dozens of soldiers were spilling out, surrounding the site and motioning them to step back. The noise was so great that there was no point trying to protest.

Dad and the twins retreated all the way back to the canal bridge and watched as the soldiers began roping off the area and erecting screens around the Angel's head.

"Looks like they know what's in there, then," said Dad.

"Like what?" asked Joe.

"Well, it was a bad storm last night, but there was still an exercise on the Plain," continued Dad. "My best bet would be someone missed their target."

As they stood talking, it became clear their continued presence had been noted. One of the soldiers was striding towards them on the other side of the canal.

"Excuse me sir," he addressed Dad. "Best to take your children away from the area for their own safety."

"Oh, is it a bomb, then?" chipped in Em mischievously, always angry to be referred to as a "child".

"I don't know nothing about no bomb, Miss," snapped the soldier. "In these parts it's best to leave the army to get on with what they need to do. I'd forget what you've seen and go about your business if I were you." And with that he turned on his heels and strode back towards his colleagues.

"I think that's 'Get lost!' in soldier-speak," said Joe, the others' silence confirming their agreement.

As they slowly walked away, Dad looked over his shoulder at the soldiers on the hillside in the distance: "Little green men, indeed," he murmured.

CHAPTER 3
WATCH YOUR STEP

With a clean and orderly house and nothing much to do, Anna decided now was as good a time as any to get out and meet the neighbours.

The obvious place to start was the dairy farm next door, the one with the array of farm machinery that kept J busy at the window for mercifully long periods. Anna had to remind herself that, despite the fact that she'd been up for hours, for other people it was still extremely early, but the farmhouse's windows were fully lit and the curtains drawn so she thought she'd take her chances.

With J in his new waterproof overalls and Thomas the Tank Engine wellies, they strolled across the farmyard hand in hand. Almost immediately a smiling face appeared at the nearest window of the farmhouse and Anna breathed an internal sigh of relief; this was going to be easier than she had expected.

Mrs Frost, it turned out, was a widow with several strapping sons who ran the farm for her whilst she kept them fed and watered, no mean feat in itself. After a cup of tea at the long, oak kitchen table she offered Anna a quick tour of the farm, which she willingly accepted.

This was the sort of person she remembered from her childhood: open, friendly and welcoming, with time to spend talking and sharing the details of their lives.

She knew, of course, that the locals wouldn't consider her an outsider. Born in the area, word had already got around what her maiden name was and the connection made to her parents in the neighbouring village. As her husband liked to point out, the tribal drums still beat strongly out here.

"Come and see the baby calves, dear," she said to J, who toddled happily after her. Thirty minutes later, after J had sat in a tractor and been shown a combine harvester in the barn, they left Mrs Frost's with a small churn of fresh, creamy milk and an open invitation to bring the whole family to tea.

***

"So what did you find up on the hill, then?" asked Mum as Dad and the twins trudged into the kitchen.

"Well the good news is they didn't manage to bomb the village," smiled Dad thinly.

"What?" shrieked Mum, producing an immediate whine from J.

"Well, there's a big hole and a lot of chalk blown out of the hillside and a bunch of army boys in helicopters telling people to mind their own business. Looks like a cock-up to me."

"I know!" said Em, running for her camera. "Let's take some photos of it! Maybe the newspapers would be interested in them!"

"Too late," called Joe, turning from the window. "They've already covered it up with camouflage netting." Em slowly walked back across the kitchen, having spotted she'd trailed mud across the floor and hoping no-one else had noticed.

"Look," said Mum, trying to regain control of the situation, "we've only just got here, we don't really know anyone yet so let's not rock the boat, OK?" Her words were met with three shrugs and mumbled agreement. She momentarily remembered wondering one day whether she hadn't got three teenagers on her hands. She deftly changed the subject.

"Well, while you've all been out ... exploring, J and I went next door and met Mrs Frost and her cows. Lovely lady, she gave us this."

"What is it?" asked Joe, unimpressed.

"It's a little milk churn of proper fresh milk. You've got to try some, it tastes like no milk you've ever tasted." She sighed. "It's perfect! This is just the sort of new experience I wanted you all to have."

Her three teenagers glanced momentarily at each other and then out of the window to the khaki patch on the hillside. She pretended not to notice.

***

A mist blew across the stable-yard muffling the serene passage of an impossibly tall, black-cloaked figure with a gleaming scythe. An outstretched bony finger tapped a gentle rhythm on the window pane, his voice a sigh that spoke of infinite suffering:

> *The Angel came from Heaven and she whispered in my ear*

*"A plague will come upon you but you two shall
have no fear.
You will look up towards me and the Moon and
stars will shine
The road to truth is hard to tread but peace will
soon be thine."*

Em sat bolt upright in bed panting hard, her body
drenched in a cold sweat. A high-pitched scream of pain
made her leap from her bed and fling open the bedroom
door.

"It's J," yawned Joe, standing dazed in the corridor.
"He's been monumentally sick. Projectile vomited
across his duvet. Dad wants to take him to casualty but
Mum says it's miles away. Are you all right?" he added,
noticing the sweat dripping down her forehead.

"Just a stupid nightmare," she shivered. "I'll change
and see if Mum wants any help."

***

The end of another sleep-deprived night saw them all
bright and early in the nearest GP's surgery waiting for
an emergency appointment for J. Mum having phoned
ahead, they'd all come along to register, another
formality that needed to be got out of the way.

"Master Priest?" called a tall, hearty figure from the
corridor, resplendent in a pale blue bow-tie over a pink
shirt and red cords. At the sight of him, Anna cringed
inwardly and hoped her husband wasn't about to
alienate their new family doctor with one of his so-
called "jokes" that strangers always seemed to interpret
as personal insults. Fortunately he seemed lost for

words. Before he could find any, Anna stood up with J in her arms and followed the doctor into his consulting room.

Em and Joe were soon called by other doctors for an "introductory health-check" and then sent to the nurse for blood tests. Once Mum and Dad had come back with J, it was their turn for a check up and blood letting.

"So what did he say's wrong with J, then?" asked Em when they were all back in the car.

"Well, he asked us a lot of questions," said Dad slowly "like 'Has he been in contact with livestock recently?' and 'Could he have eaten any raw food, say unpasteurised milk?'!"

"Oh shut up, Kim!" snapped Mum from the passenger seat. "Don't you think I feel bad enough all ready?" There was an icy pause.

"Sorry love," said Dad sheepishly. "He said it was probably very mild food poisoning and we weren't to worry. J's going to have the squits for a few days but that's about it. Oh, and we all need to make sure we wash our hands very thoroughly. We're in the country now. The place is full of sh ... germs. So that means all muddy boots *must* get left in the porch from now on. Are you listening Joe?"

"Uhuh," said Joe, shooting a withering glance at his sister, who smiled back sweetly and fluttered her eyelashes sarcastically.

There was another uncomfortable pause. "I'll say one thing about the countryside, though," continued Dad, desperately trying to find something to redeem himself with his wife, "that was the most thorough check-up I've ever been given at a GP's office. I haven't given that much blood since my rugby-playing days."

31

***

They were all too tired to express much surprise at a police car parked in the stable yard when they got home. Dad got out just in time to see a tall, thickset, sandy-haired young Constable come around the side of the building. "Good morning, officer. Can we help you?" he enquired as good-naturedly as possible.

"Ah, good morning to you too, sir," said the policeman with a distinct burr in his voice. "Can I take it you're the new tenants here?"

"Yes, that's right."

"Would you mind if I came in for a moment, sir?"

"Er, no, no, not at all," said Dad a little doubtfully now, opening the door and waving the policeman in. "After you."

After hovering awkwardly in the hallway for a moment, the tall, blue figure removed his helmet and walked into the kitchen.

"Please take a seat, officer," said Mum calmly. "Can I offer you a cup of tea?"

"That would me most welcome, ma'am," said the policeman. "Milk, one sugar please."

Dad ushered the twins into the sitting room with J and made his best "Crikey! What have we done now?" expression, before closing the door behind him and settling down at the kitchen table opposite their unexpected guest.

After a few pleasantries about the weather and once he'd taken a long sip of his tea, the policeman finally came to the point: "Can I ask you, sir, whether you were

32

out on the hillside with your children yesterday morning?"

"Yes, you can," smiled Kim "and yes, we were."

"I see, sir," said the officer gravely.

"Is that a problem?" frowned Kim. "I mean is it private property or something? We followed a footpath and there were no signs so we thought ..."

"Would you mind telling me what you saw, sir?" the officer continued.

"Well, it looked like a round crater and some chalk debris that had been thrown out of it."

"Anything else, sir?"

"Er, well apart from all the soldiers, no, I don't think so."

"Did you remove anything from the site?" asked the policeman.

"No, certainly not!" said Kim, angrily. And then after a moment's thought he asked: "Why, *did* someone take something?"

"I really couldn't say, sir," the officer said, a little too dismissively for Anna's liking. He stood up to go. "Well, I hope I haven't troubled you too much with my questions," he concluded. "I would ask, however, that you don't discuss this matter with anyone else for the time being, given this it is an ongoing enquiry. Thanks again for the tea, ma'am. I'll let myself out." And before either Anna or Kim could say another word, he'd gone.

A millisecond or so passed before Em and Joe burst into the kitchen. "What did he want?" they chorused.

"Apparently someone stole something from up on the hillside yesterday and we're not to talk about what we saw to anyone," summarised Dad in an irate monotone.

"But we didn't see anything," said Em.

"Maybe we did," said Joe, thoughtfully, "but we just didn't know what it was we were looking at."

At the sound of the police car's ignition, they all turned to watch the car leave the stableyard.

"It doesn't matter what we saw anyway," added Dad pointing out of the other window at the freshly-turfed hillside. "The soldiers have flown and so has our Angel."

***

It wasn't until that afternoon that Em noticed that all their walking boots were missing from the rear porch.

"So what is it you're saying exactly, Em?" asked Mum incredulously. "A policeman stole our boots?"

"Well, it's an odd coincidence, don't you think?" countered Em.

"No odder than reading *The War of the Worlds* and seeing Mars one day and then having something crash land outside your house the next," said Joe.

"Oh *please*," said Em, exasperated. "Don't tell me you think aliens crashed into that hill?"

"Stranger things have happened," mumbled Joe, abashed.

"Like what?"

"Well our boots have walked off on their own, for a start," chipped in Dad. "Actually, love, I think Em might have a point. You said yourself that the crime rate is virtually nil around here. Maybe he borrowed them but forgot to mention it."

Anna thought for a moment. "OK, let's just suppose for one minute that he took them. What do you want *me* to do about it?"

"Well, I don't think he particularly warmed to me," understated Dad. "Perhaps you could phone the local station and ask for them back?" Anna knew she'd never hear the last of it until she had, and still felt that she was required to justify the countryside and its mysterious ways to her husband and children. She went away to phone.

"Have either of you read *The Hound of the Baskervilles*?" asked Dad.

"No, but something tells me you're going to tell us all about it," groaned Joe.

"Well," carried on Dad, ignoring his son, "Sherlock Holmes gets involved in a case when the heir to a great fortune's boots are stolen. Anyway, it turns out that the baddy wants to get something with his scent on it so he can set a huge ferocious dog on him to frighten him to death."

"Thanks, Dad," said Em sarcastically "that really helps to put my mind at rest."

"Oh, it's worse than that," grinned Dad fiendishly, doing his best creepy voice. "Have you noticed just how many people in this village own dogs?"

Mum entered the room slowly.

"So, what did they say, darling?" smiled Dad.

"Oh, well it's um, rather odd actually," she said hesitantly. "I'm sure it's some mistake. I described him and gave them his number but they say they've never heard of him."

CHAPTER 4
STRANGENESS IN THE NIGHT

In a world of uncertainties, only one thing was inevitable: Mum's PMT was back and, as usual, it meant business.

"Save yourselves kids," whispered Dad to the twins as he sneaked into the kitchen one morning. "The Minstrel's on the loose! It's seen me but there's still a chance for you."

"The Minstrel" was Dad's pet name for Mum in full-on time-of-the-month mode. The name came about as a result of J overhearing Mum asking the doctor, unsuccessfully, for some help with her menstrual pain, and then having to spend the rest of the day listening to him shouting "Mummy minstrel" at the top of his voice all over town. Dad thought this was hilarious, Mum less so.

Em and Joe didn't need telling twice. Dad shoved a few banknotes in their hands and pointed at the windows and doors in a comic imitation of an air-hostess: "You'll find the emergency exits here, here and here. Good luck! Oh, and buy yourself some more walking boots if you get the chance."

***

Barely five minutes passed before Em and Joe met up in the yard and started walking towards the main road.

"Good to get out of the house," said Joe after a while. "It's like J's a real sweetie, you know, but his nappies are totally rank. When did Mum say he'd be better again?"

"Could be a week," replied Em. "Things could get a lot worse if he passes it on the rest of us. Maybe it's time you started flushing the loo and washing your hands properly?" she added pointedly.

"Yeah, whatever," grunted Joe.

Silence again.

"So where are we going, then?" asked Joe. "It's miles into town. Typical, isn't it! Dad gives us a wad of cash and there's nowhere to spend it."

"That's what you think," said Em taking out her mobile. "You're forgetting the Wigglybus."

"Are you taking the …"

"Shhh! Yes, hello," said Em into her phone. "Can you pick us up from the stop by All Cannings canal bridge, please? 20 minutes? Yeah, that's fine thanks. Seeya!"

"What just happened?" asked Joe.

"I ordered us a bus pick up," said Em. "I saw this sign in the library and put the number in my mobile. There's a bus that wiggles it's way around all the villages and you can call the driver to come and pick you up and take you into town."

"Oh right, and I bet it's like painted pink or something embarrassing," mumbled Joe.

"It's blue and, be honest, it's a pretty cool idea."

"So we've got 20 minutes to kill, then?" said Joe, who actually agreed it was a good idea but didn't want to give up his determinedly sulky attitude towards the countryside for the sake of a cheap ride. "What about a look at the canal, then?"

Em shrugged her agreement and they picked their way across a car park pockmarked with puddles to reach the towpath gate. A family of swans sunning themselves on the opposite bank looked up at their arrival.

Passing through the gate the twins found themselves looking left and right at a gently curving kilometre of canal barges of every size and colour moored along the towpath.

"That black one looks like a floating coffin," noted Joe.

"It's a lovely view," said Em, ignoring him as she took in the fields of waving wheat, the sheep grazing and the long line of undulating hills, like a ruffled duvet, running parallel to the canal on the north side of the valley. "Oh, and look!" she added, pointing west. "There's that white horse on the hillside Mum was talking about."

They wandered a short way along the towpath, watching a few barges chug by, their drivers perched at the rear, tiller beneath one hand and a mug of tea or a sandwich in the other. "Looks like fun," said Em, who having had time to think about it, had decided it was time to accept her fate and make the most of her new surroundings.

"Maybe," said Joe, "but I don't think I'd fancy a family trip in one of them."

"Don't knock it 'til you've tried it, mate!" came a disembodied voice. A dreadlocked head of indeterminate years poked out of the little doors at the front of the nearest barge. "Name's Daz. What's yours?" the head said, introducing itself.

"Em."

"Joe."

"Hi! You live around here?" asked Daz.

"No, well yes, I suppose so," stumbled Em.

"Know how you feel," chuckled Daz. "D'ya want to come aboard?"

Joe looked at Em doubtfully but she shrugged back and climbed into the prow of the boat. Joe followed reluctantly. "Tea?" asked Daz. Joe caught a heady waft of patchouli oil, something some of his longer-haired classmates, who were rumoured to be doing drugs, reeked of. He decided to decline the offer, wondering what the "tea" might turn out to be.

"So," said Em after a pause, "do you live on the boat all the time?"

"Oh, yeah," said Daz, "I came down here for the summer solstice at Stonehenge one year and decided I couldn't ever leave. There's so much energy in the landscape here, you know, it just pulls you in."

"Oh really?" said Joe sarcastically. Daz seemed not to have noticed.

"Oh yeah. I mean the ley lines around here are like spaghetti junction. Do you know there's one going straight down the main street here that runs from Avebury to Stonehenge, man. That's like the spiritual M1."

"So what does that mean, exactly?" said Em.

"It means it's a magical place and a lot of weird things happen round here." Joe and Em exchanged a glance. "Hey, you know what I'm talking about, right?"

"Did you see the Angel?" asked Em.

"The what?" asked Daz. Em explained. "Woah, that's a good one!" said Daz excitedly. Then his face dropped. "Bummer! I always miss the good stuff! Listen. Some of my mates are coming down here to see me later on and they'd love to hear this. Can you come back this evening, say about eight?"

"OK, if you really want us to," said Em casually, secretly excited to be of so much interest.

"There's our bus," said Joe suddenly, relieved to have an excuse to get away.

"By the way," said Daz as they got up to leave "I wouldn't bother talking to the locals about this. Half of them are army or ex-army and the rest married to them. What they know, they won't tell you and what they don't know, they don't wanna know."

***

The Wigglybus lived up to its name, taking an unfathomable route into Devizes that neither of them could follow. After a quick hunt round the shoe shops for more boots, they soon found themselves outside the library again.

"What do you want in here?" asked Joe. "You've already got out more books than I've ever read."

"Which isn't saying much," smirked Em. "I just want a quick surf to find out some more about all that stuff Daz was saying."

"Oh no," said Joe in a suspicious tone. "You're not actually planning to go back and talk to him and his weirdo mates tonight, are you?"

"He's not 'weird', he's 'alternative'. We don't all have to live exactly the same lives you know," said Em, suppressing a momentary cringe as she realised she sounded like Mum ticking Dad off. "Anyway," she hurried on, "I won't be going alone."

"Why didn't I see that one coming?" sighed Joe. "OK, I'll come with you, but if they try to read my aura or start on the wacky baccy, I'm out of there."

A few minutes later the twins were sitting side by side tapping words into search engines, Em looking up Avebury, Stonehenge and ley lines and Joe tapping in whatever came to mind. From time to time Em would tell Joe what she'd found out and he'd grunt in acknowledgement.

"It says here that they now think that Stonehenge is there to indicate the winter solstice and the end of winter and not the longest day, which is when all the hippies and the TV reporters turn up to bother the druids."

"Uh huh."

"This website says that Avebury is three huge stone circles set out in the shape of a snake passing through them and that they're over 4,500 years old!"

"Hmm!"

"Apparently this leyline thing is all about some guy who reckoned that all these stone circles and ancient monuments are linked together by straight lines in the landscape. They go for hundreds of miles. Oh, and Daz was right, there is one major one with Avebury at the top and Stonehenge at the bottom that passes straight through All Cannings!"

"Hmm."

After a while Em turned to him and asked: "Are you actually listening to me?"

"Have you ever heard of Porton Down?" Joe replied.

"Er, no," said Em. "Should I have? What is it?"

"Well I was thinking about J, so I tapped in 'poisoning' and 'Wiltshire' and all this stuff came up about it," said Joe. "It's a military research place just up the road from here that's made loads of chemical and biological weapons. It says here that they used to experiment on soldiers giving them all this stuff but telling them they were looking for a cure for the common cold."

"Is there any good news?" asked Em.

"Well, it says here they stopped experimenting on the soldiers years ago after word got out that one of them had died."

"Mmm, cheery! Thanks for that!" said Em. "Look, I think I've had just about as much as I can take of bacteria and viruses for one day."

"Fair enough!" agreed Joe hopping to his feet. "Let's go to that Italian café we passed over by the supermarket. Looked clean enough!"

***

After a hasty dinner, prepared by Dad, as Mum lurked upstairs in her room like Mrs Rochester in *Jane Eyre* (a book Mum had lent Em to read), the twins declared they were off for a walk and might watch the sunset, much to Dad's surprise.

"Well OK then, have fun," he said with a hint of abandonment. "If you get lost out there, give me a ring and I'll come and find you."

"Yeah, right!" scoffed Joe. Dad's appalling sense of direction was legendary.

Daz's friends, as it turned out, were pretty normal in a nerdy sort of way. Just a couple of guys and girls in their late teens or early twenties, Em judged, who all wore glasses and T shirts with stuff like *Red Dwarf, Star Trek* and *Stargate* on them. If she'd had to hazard a guess, she'd have said they'd all be pretty good at maths and have some serious computer kit at home.

They were setting up a barbecue on the towpath as Em and Joe approached. The twins soon accepted a couple of cans of Coke from a cool box whilst Daz made the introductions. There was Dave, Bob, Becky and Fay but it wasn't easy to work out who was with who, or if they were couples at all.

Once they were all settled down on various plastic chairs and cushions from the barge, Daz asked Em to tell everyone about the Angel.

"I don't really want to talk too loud about this," she half-whispered, forcing them all to lean forward expectantly, much to her unintended delight. Once she had finished, they all sat back and silence reigned for all of a millisecond.

"Wicked story!" said Bob, impressed.

"What did I tell you," said Daz, pleased.

"Yeah, brilliant! You ought to be a writer or something," said Dave.

Em blushed. "Er, thanks, but I was really just telling it like it happened."

"Really weird though the army turning up like that and then the police guy stealing your shoes," said Becky. "Maybe you trod in something."

"Well, there's a lot of stuff to tread in around here," quipped Joe, but no-one laughed.

"Yeah, maybe it was radioactive or something," said Fay in her light, otherworldly voice.

"Oh, here we go," said Dave with a snort. "May the meeting of the Conspiracy Theorists and Associated Whackos come to order."

"Now I don't think that's exactly fair," began Daz.

"It's OK, Daz," sighed Fay wearily "I'm used to having my beliefs doubted."

"Actually," said Becky "Fay might have a point. If the army dropped a bomb or whatever on the hillside, maybe it had something nasty in it. What about all that stuff about D.U. being used on Salisbury Plain you read on the net, Bob?"

"Er, what's D.U.?" asked Em, hesitantly.

"D.U., Depleted Uranium," said Bob in his nerdy nasal voice. "It's like old fuel rods from nuclear reactors. It's a really heavy metal so they put it in bombs and missiles to give them extra punch."

"I think we should change the subject," said Becky in a concerned voice "I think we're upsetting Joe." They all turned to look at him, sitting with his hands over his mouth.

"Don't worry about me," he said sulkily, "I was just trying not to yawn."

"Right!" said Daz, quickly changing the subject. "So who's up for a little walk then?"

"Little walk?" asked Em, dubiously, looking at the setting sun.

"Oh, it's all right, Em," smiled Becky "There's nothing to worry about. This lot are *totally* harmless."

"Yeah, taking a walk could be a good idea," said Joe pointedly in Em's direction, a hint she decided to ignore.

"Good!" said Daz. "I've got a really good route mapped out." And so off they went.

***

They walked in the warm summer air with the soothing chirruping of crickets in the long grass, Joe talking to Fay no doubt, thought Em, so he could have something to snigger about tomorrow. Em chatted to Becky, who insisted she really had to visit Old Sarum, a massive ancient earthwork fort near Salisbury.

"Here we are, then!" said Daz turning suddenly at the front of the group. "Now where did I leave that bag?" He rummaged around in the blackness near a hedgerow. Suddenly a pen torch came on in his right hand lighting up a long green, canvas bag with what looked like a lot of rope and boards in it. Em instinctively reached out and grasped Joe's arm.

"So where's the plan, Bob?" asked Dave, as Bob clicked on his own torch and unfolded a large sheet of squared paper from his back pocket. "Cool! Is that a fractal?"

"Yeah, nice work Bob!" added Daz. "It's gonna take us hours though. Best get to it."

The little group of friends gathered round Bob and Daz, looking at the plan and unravelling the ropes. Em and Joe stood off to one side.

"Er, what are you doing exactly?" Em asked eventually.

"Isn't it obvious?" said Fay, who was nearest to them. "We're making a crop circle."

Em and Joe stood in stunned silence for a moment as the various pen torches sliced through the darkening air around them.

"But you said you had 'beliefs'?" said Joe, too surprised to be sarcastic.

"It's a complex field …," began Daz.

"Or it's going to be when we've finished!" quipped Dave, to a chorus of groans.

"Some people think they're signs from another world," continued Daz, "others that they're caused by freak weather. All we know is that they're a lot of fun!"

"That's not all," added Fay loftily. "I like to think we're responding to some higher calling …"

Joe's phone bleeped as it received a text message. He looked at Em. "I dunno about 'higher callings'," he said sarcastically, "but Dad wants to know if we're coming home yet."

***

Back at the house, Kim's mobile vibrated on the kitchen table as he made some hot cocoa for Anna to help her sleep.

"Where are they?" said Anna sharply. She was sitting at the far end of the table, with her head in her hands.

"It's OK," said Dad, reading the text. "They're absolutely fine. They got a little lost but they're on their way back now."

He sat down beside his wife and held one of her hands. "Do you remember that conversation we had before we moved here about learning to give them more space and to let them off the lead a bit more? Well, if we can't do it out here, where can we?"

"Kim, do you remember what life was like when you were their age?" Anna asked.

"Yes, I think so," Kim smiled back. "It was all music, mates, exams and thinking a lot about the opposite sex."

"Yes, but do you remember the feeling of boundless energy and of everything being so new, so exciting and just waiting to be discovered?"

"Yeah, I loved those girls!" Kim laughed.

"I am *trying* to make a serious point here," Anna almost growled.

"Sorry," he said, somewhat cowed.

"But looking back on it now, I can see we were also a bit clueless. We had no real sense of danger and we'd believe virtually anything. Our parents warned us against this or that but somehow it just made whatever it was more exciting and egg us on to try it all the more."

"So what are you saying?" asked Dad.

"I'm worried what they might get involved in."

"Do you honestly think that your parents, my parents and probably every parent who ever lived hasn't had this precise conversation at some point or other?" Kim asked, sympathetically. "They're growing up and that's something we can't stop. All we can do is try to guide them the best way we can, as gently as we can. You don't want their last few years living with us to be all about conflict and boundaries, do you?"

Anna opened her mouth to speak again but checked herself. After a pause she said: "Letting them go is going to be so hard."

"I know." He kissed her hand. She smiled thinly.

"And so is accepting that you're right, damn you."

"Yeah, that really stings, doesn't it," he grinned. "And anyway, they're *our* kids, they're not stupid."

"Yes," said Anna, doubtfully "that's exactly what I'm worried about."

***

"Do you have any idea where you're going?" asked Em for the third time in as many minutes.

"No," replied Joe finally, striding briskly through the corn field.

"We didn't come this way before did we?" continued Em.

"No," replied Joe tersely, still striding on. A steady cool wind had got up behind them and Em was shivering in her thin summer clothes.

"Would you just stop for a minute, please?" demanded Em. Joe stopped and turned to face her. She could just make out his features in the pale moonlight.

"What are you so angry about?" she asked.

"I really hate liars," he said simply. "The whole world seems to be full of people lying to other people. You want to believe in things, you know? New, exciting and interesting things like Mum always wants us to, and then you discover that it's all a lie, just some bunch of idiots thinking they're all so damned clever for fooling everyone else."

As he spoke, the clouds cleared from the Moon and Em looked around.

"Do you realise where we're standing?" she asked. Joe looked about in the faint light.

"Is this one they made earlier?" he said sarcastically as he surveyed the line of crop circles they were standing right in the centre of.

"I don't know," replied Em, "but whatever you think of the people who make them, you have to admit, they're pretty cool to look at."

"All I see is a load of good food ruined by mindless vandals," snapped Joe.

"It's pretty neat work though," went on Em, crouching down by the corn at the edge of the nearest shape, and feeling a brief sensation of relief as she sheltered from the cold wind.

As she began to stand up, though, her senses told her, all within a split second, that something wasn't right. First she turned her head slightly and sniffed the air. Then she noticed an odd crackling sound and felt a sudden rise in temperature on her face. The flicker of light from the edge of the cornfield upwind and a glimpse of a tall, dark figure through the heat haze put the last piece of the puzzle in place.

"Run!" she shouted, "Something's wrong!"

"What?" asked Joe.

"A fire! There! Someone's set the field alight!"

As Joe turned to look, the flames were already ripping across the crops, flicked by the gathering breeze.

After a moment's stunned immobility, his adrenalin kicked in and he was soon keeping pace with Em as she sprinted through the corn. The chill breeze at their backs now felt like a burning Saharan wind, the smoke thickening and making them choke as they gulped in air to keep on running.

"This way!" wheezed Joe, grabbing Em's wrist and turning at a right angle to their current direction. "We've got to get out of the field!"

For a split second Em considered arguing but there was no time. The wind was whipping the flames and the smoke ever nearer and the heat was so intense that to stand still was impossible. She covered the side of her head and face with her arm to protect them from the heat and charged after Joe.

He was right! Fifty metres in front of them there was a wide ditch and a road beyond. They flung themselves at the far bank of the ditch, scrabbling up onto the tarmac surface, and kept running. After a few hundred metres they passed a signpost back to the village and finally slackened their pace.

"What … what happened?" Joe finally got out between deep breaths, massaging a stitch and gratefully swallowing big gulps of the cool night air.

"I … dunno," wheezed Em, still coughing a little from the smoke. "I thought I saw someone."

They stood, regaining their breath for a while and looking back at the glow of the flaming field and the ghostly plumes of smoke rising into the night sky.

"Let's get out of here," said Joe, eventually. "We've already had the police round just because we went for a walk. Can you imagine what they'll do to us if they think we've burned their crops?"

CHAPTER 5
ESCAPE

August was a scorching month. The combine harvesters worked endlessly in the fields and the revving and metallic clanking of the farm machinery next door began early in the morning and continued long into the night. The grain drier went into overdrive and was all the louder now they were sleeping with the windows open.

"D'ya know," said Dad one morning at breakfast to a chorus of sniffing, "if I'd know we'd all have hay fever I'd have suggested moving to the seaside instead."

"You did," snuffled Em darkly.

"Yeah, Mum wouldn't let us," added Joe.

"Do you lot ever stop moaning?" asked Mum. Her words met a wall of sulky silence. "Well, it was going to be a surprise for your Dad's birthday but I've booked us a fortnight in Lyme Regis."

"Where?" chorused the twins.

"It's a seaside resort on the Dorset coast. Your Dad used to go there when he was a lad."

"No way!" said Joe "Are you sure it's still there?"

"Less of your cheek, young man!" said Dad, making a grab for Joe's cheek as he struggled away.

"Gerroff, Dad!"

"Children, children!" called Mum.

"So when are we off?" sniffed Em, grumpily. "Soon I hope."

"This Saturday soon enough for you?" asked Mum.

"What?" whined Em. "But I haven't even got a bikini or anything!"

"It's OK, I've already thought of that. I'm taking you shopping in Bath on Wednesday." Kim groaned.

"Of course, if your father doesn't want any birthday presents this year ..." continued Mum.

"OK! Go if you must," said Dad raising his hands in surrender, "just go easy on the credit cards."

***

Saturday began beautifully, the sun rising over the farmhouse as the centrepiece of a pastel-shaded dream of pink and blue stripes emanating from the eastern horizon. For once, Anna and J were the only ones to see it, as the others all rolled over to enjoy another precious half hour in bed.

"Tea up!" Mum cried at the bottom of the stairs and three groans signalled that the rest of the house was now awake.

With the carrot of a sandy beach dangling in front of them, Joe and Dad loaded the car in record time and were soon tooting the horn impatiently.

"Women!" sighed Dad, strapping J into his child seat. "I've been married to your mother for donkeys years, but I still don't know what it is women actually do between the time they *say* they're coming and when they eventually deign to arrive."

"Preserving an air of mystery?" suggested Joe.

"That's possible," conceded Dad. "Personally, I'd always thought they were on the loo."

"Yeah, great. Thanks, Dad!" said Joe. "Nice image!"

"Sorry, son!"

A window opened and out popped Em's head. "Mum says it's quite a long way, so don't forget to go before we leave." Joe and Dad looked at each other and laughed. "I don't know why I bother," said Em, closing the window again.

***

The "holiday home" turned out to be almost too good to be true. Mum had obviously decided to push the boat out for Dad's birthday and had hired a massive six bedroom house with an enormous garden overlooking Lyme Bay.

"Wow!" seemed to be the only word anyone said for the first ten minutes after they had crunched up the wide gravelled driveway. It was an art deco masterpiece: white walls, curved windows, a spiral staircase leading up to an enclosed sun terrace above a triple garage. Em almost expected a butler to open the wide oak door.

As they stood in the centre of the front lawn taking it all in, Em put her arm through Anna's. "This is just fantastic but I don't get it. How can we afford it?"

"Well, I haven't told your father yet, but the Grands and Aunt Mary are coming to stay with us for the second week, so they've chipped in to deaden the pain a little."

"Do you think he'll mind?" asked Em.

"Are you kidding?" smiled Mum. "He's thrilled! He hasn't been silent this long since the first time we …" and she raised her eyebrows significantly and laughed.

"Eww, Mum!" said Em, pulling a face, "Sometimes you give me *way* too much information."

***

The town was no less inspiring. A dramatically steep high street of bustling little boutiques, old-fashioned newsagents, sweet shops and greengrocers led down to a long promenade beside a narrow pebble and sand beach. At one end were what looked like battlements defending the town's theatre and museum, whilst at the other the resort's famous harbour and its defensive wall, The Cobb, snaked out into the sea.

The family lost no time in pitching their sun tent, laying out their towels and slapping on the sun cream. Em lay resplendent in her new designer bikini and sunglasses, lapping up admiring glances and feeling a million dollars. Mum and Dad sat in hired deckchairs, Mum with her latest novel, Dad with his newspaper, and Joe and J made endless holes and sandcastles. A gentle breeze blew seagulls and puffy white clouds across a deep blue sky and life was perfect.

***

By the end of the fourth day, Em, and everyone else, had noticed that one particular boy was walking past an awful lot, enough for Dad to comment: "Well, either he fancies you Em or he's got a very bad case of the runs."

In the end, however, something about him started to bother Kim.

"OK!" he said, jumping up from his seat "Who's for an ice-cream?" to be met by a chorus of small cheers. "Right, so that's two chocolates, a raspberry ripple, a 'storbry' for J and whatever I'm having." And then he added as an afterthought. "Come to think of it, I'll need a hand to carry them. Em, would you mind, love? OK, we'll be back in a mo!" He had timed his movements perfectly and they slotted in unperceived to follow the lad back up the beach.

The boy, a little older than Em, Kim judged, walked past the loos ("Wrong again!" thought Kim), past the ice-cream stand and went to sit with a couple and a young girl at a seafront café. Kim hesitated for a moment and then, just as he was hovering, deciding what to do next, the blonde woman at the table looked up and said:

"Kim? Kim, is that really you?"

"Sally?" exclaimed Kim in astonishment.

"Kim!" she turned to the man "Look, Ralph it's Kim." The look on the man's face first registered shock, then he masterfully gathered his emotions and stood up smiling, extending his right hand.

"Kim, old man, how are you?" somewhat reluctantly, Em thought.

"Fine thanks, Ralph." Kim managed to sound pleased and thought he'd got away with it.

"And this is Tom and Natasha," continued Ralph, indicating the young lad and his younger sister.

"Hello!"

"Hi!"

There was a pause until Em elbowed Kim, who was just standing, smiling dopily at Sally.

"Oh, er yes," he stuttered, remembering himself, "this is my daughter, Em."

"Hi!" said Em, risking a quick glance at Tom who was doing the same at her and clearly feeling as awkward as she was.

"God! What's it been? Almost twenty years?" continued Sally excitedly. Kim nodded. "So what are you doing *here*?"

"My birthday week holiday," explained Kim.

"Of course! I'd completely forgotten!" She turned to Ralph. "Kim's parents always timed their summer holiday to coincide with his birthday. I came here with them once."

"Yes, I remember you telling me," said Ralph with the thinnest of smiles. His unblinking, dark eyes had not left Kim's.

"Gosh! What an elephant you are!" laughed Sally. "Imagine remembering that!"

There was a hardness in Ralph's gaze and Em was thrilled to see that there was clearly some history here; she was going to enjoy finding out all about it!

Kim noticed Ralph's gaze too, and thought he was plainly the sort of man who stored away every little detail about his enemies, and probably his friends too.

"Won't you join us? We could get some more chairs?" said Ralph, but both Kim and Em could read the message in his eyes loud and clear: "GO AWAY!"

"No, no, really, the others are waiting for us," Kim smiled to Sally.

"Oh you're not getting away that easily," purred Sally. "Come and have lunch with us tomorrow. We're staying at Church Cliff."

"Oh, we wouldn't want to intrude …" began Kim.

"Nonsense! The children don't know anyone here. They'd love to have someone else to play with." It was plain Sally wasn't taking "no" for an answer. "Here's my mobile number," she scribbled on an edge of the menu, tore it off and handed it to Kim. "Shall we say around one o'clock?"

"Well, OK, that'd be lovely," Kim said, feeling Ralph's eyes burning into the side of his head.

As they walked back towards the ice-cream stand, Em took Dad's hand. "So who was that then?" she grinned, enjoying her Dad's discomfort.

"An old girlfriend and her extremely jealous husband," said Dad flatly.

"And are we really going to have lunch with them?"

"I think we should let your Mum decide," said Kim, doubtfully.

***

Em thought that Mum took Dad's news of bumping into an old girlfriend extremely well. She wasn't so keen on having to socialise with her, however:

"Oh Lord! Do we have to, Kim?"

"It's entirely up to you, darling," said Kim, his hands raised in mock surrender.

"Oh, thanks!" said Anna. "If I say no, we have to spend the rest of the holiday looking over our shoulder and trying to avoid them, and if I say yes …"

Kim shrugged: "What's the worst that could happen?"

57

"Ralph might kill you?" suggested Em, looking up from her magazine.

"Oh really?" said Mum, interestedly. "Well in *that* case, perhaps this could be more fun than I thought!"

***

As J tended to sleep over lunchtime, Mum decided to suggest an evening meal instead. A phone call was made and the swap arranged.

They duly arrived at Church Cliff the following evening in their best clothes and carrying their contribution to a barbecue. Em had on the expensive new summer dress Mum had bought her in Bath (another pleasant surprise for Dad!).

Sally and Ralph's house was a modern three-storey effort of glass, wood and steel, clearly inspired by an ocean-going liner. Buzzed in by Sally via the intercom, they clanked up the wrought iron spiral staircase to the wide roof-terrace with its glass-sided balcony giving an uninterrupted, 360-degree view of the town, the bay and the sea.

Ralph was standing stiffly behind the barbecue in a starched blue and white striped apron, with a murderous look on his face and a large kitchen knife in his hand, which he was using to separate some frozen beef burgers. Sally rushed forward to meet them:

"How wonderful you could come!" she gushed. Dad made the introductions. Joe and Tom nodded at each other. Em and Natasha exchanged smiles.

"Nice place you have here," Anna said.

"Oh, it's nothing really," said Sally "just a hangover from Ralph's youth. He learned to sail here when he was a child."

"Oh really?" smiled Anna, "Well so did I, so I'll go over and help him with the barbecue and give you two a chance to catch up."

As she moved away, Tom and Em's eyes met and their mutual embarrassment at the situation was palpable. What could be more cringe-worthy than watching one of your parents with an old flame?

"Would you like to look around?" asked Tom.

***

The evening went surprisingly smoothly. Mum was clearly up to placating Ralph whilst Dad and Sally reminisced, and was obviously enjoying herself as she was quite happy for Em and Joe to share a Budweiser and even try some of her wine.

As a sunset like an oil painting stood in the west and a sprinkling of stars appeared in the east, the parents moved to a line of easy chairs in one corner of the terrace to enjoy the view. Joe and Natasha had discovered a mutual interest in videogames and went off to play Natasha's latest favourite.

"Would you like to go for a walk on the beach?" asked Tom. "We could watch the sunset from there if you like."

After a quick glance over towards Mum, who gave her a little wink, Em agreed.

***

The east end of the beach was a lot more pebbly than the sand-filled curve near the Cobb and Tom was soon holding Em's hand to steady her as they walked out to see the rock pools uncovered by the low tide. They walked up the stone groynes and jumped down into the sand at the water's edge and paddled in the gentle surf. Em noticed that they were still holding hands.

"We'd probably best be getting back now," she said.

"Oh I'm sorry, you must be cold in just that dress," said Tom, taking off his sweater and wrapping it round Em's shoulders. "There how's that?"

He still had hold of the sweater's sleeves and as Em looked up to answer him, he pulled them, and her, gently towards him.

His kiss was soft and warm and fuzzy (that bit was probably the alcohol). Em couldn't say how long it lasted but it could have been an eternity if a slightly larger wave hadn't crashed against them, soaking their legs. They swayed at the impact and laughed.

"Come on," said Em. "Race you back to the house!" and she shot off up the beach, the hem of her skirt in one hand and her shoes in the other, with Tom in soggy-legged pursuit.

***

"So what's all this I hear about your practical jokes at college then?" Anna asked Kim. Kim reddened slightly and looked at Ralph. He clearly had been keeping notes.

"Oh yes, he was brilliant at it!" erupted a boozily enthusiastic Sally. "Do you remember the time you

60

covered all the lecturers' loo seats in clingfilm. They went berserk! Literally wet themselves with anger!" Kim was already a little sunburned and flushed by the red wine but he was glad it was dark enough not to show his increasing blushes. "Oh, and then there was that time you and Dom held up all the traffic outside the college by pretending you were carrying a large pane of glass. They were so convincing! And of course all us girls thought they were such crazy guys!"

***

"That was hideous," Kim said to Anna as they sat in bed that night.

"Oh, don't be such a grump," smiled Anna. "It's fun to catch up with old friends."

"Huh!" grunted Kim. "I almost cheered when they said they were leaving tomorrow."

"Hmm!" said Anna thoughtfully. "I'm not sure that Em's going to share your enthusiasm."

CHAPTER 6
A GRAND OLD TIME

They woke the next morning to find Grandpa's car in the driveway.

"He always insists on leaving at the crack of dawn," moaned Grandma to Em, who opened the front door in her nightie. "Pop the kettle on, dear. On second thoughts, go and put some clothes on before you catch your death."

Em went back to bed to sleep off her hangover. Mum and Dad weren't so lucky.

***

The holiday's second week was a totally different proposition, entirely due to the new arrivals. The family's daily schedule, lax until now, became more regimented as Grandpa took charge.

"OK," he would announce after breakfast each morning, "what are our plans today?" Anyone without a clear account of their intended movements found themselves taken for one of Grandpa's "walks", which more closely resembled a route march, or for an informative visit to a museum or another local place of interest.

For Dad's birthday this year, the Grands had agreed to give Anna and Kim some time alone together. And so early one morning Em, Joe and J found themselves crunching down the long, gravel drive in Grandpa's car as Aunt Mary was setting off on foot, her easel strapped to her back, to indulge her passion for totally incomprehensible watercolours.

Grandpa always liked to retain an air of mystery and it was only after about an hour of wiggling along country roads past Axmouth, Seaton, Beer and Sidmouth that they arrived at Bicton Gardens.

As the Grands took it in turn to push J's pushchair, Em and Joe moped along behind.

"Did you ever think that if they'd just give us the money instead of dragging us off on all these days out we've had to suffer over the years, we'd be loaded by now?" asked Em wryly. They walked a little more in silence.

"I was wondering," said Joe tentatively "and you can tell me to mind my own business, but did you and Tom like er … get off the other night?" Em stopped dead and turned to look at him.

"Yes," she said and paused. "You're right, it really is none of your business." She laughed. "And if we did?"

"I was just thinking it was a bit sad if you met someone one day and the next day he's got to go home," said Joe, starting to wish he'd never started, "especially after all the hassle you had with Mike. And anyway, Mum's always saying you're my little Sis and I ought to look out for you."

"'Little Sis'?" repeated Em. "I'm not sure being older by ten minutes really counts. And anyway, something tells me I'll be seeing Tom again."

***

After a picnic lunch on one of the immaculate lawns, Gran took J for a push to get him to sleep and Em and Joe sat with Grandpa.

"Have you seen the bright blue dragonflies on the moat, Grandpa?" asked Joe.

"Yes, amazing aren't they. 'There are more things in heaven and earth ...'"

"Meaning?" asked Em.

"Well," he thought for a moment, "it means there are more things around us than we can hope to explain or know about."

"Oh," said Em, as Joe helped himself to the last piece of cake. "Grandpa," she continued "what do you know about depleted uranium?" Joe choked on the cake.

"D.U.?" repeated Grandpa. "Why would you want to know about that?"

"Well we met some people from one of the barges on the Kennet and Avon canal and they were telling us that a lot of it gets used up on Salisbury Plain."

"Oh, you don't want to worry yourself about that," said Grandpa kindly. "I was talking to Old Buffy about it only the other night and he said that the whole issue had been blown out of all proportion by the media."

"Old Buffy?" asked Joe.

"Buffy Harris, lives in All Cannings, up at the Bastion," said Grandpa. "Anyway, he ought to know about such things. Not only was he in charge of all

64

operations on the Plain when I first met him but he went on to be a big cheese at Porton Down, apparently. All very hush-hush!" he winked. "Have you finished that cake yet, Joe?" he added.

"Hmm!" replied Joe stuffing the last half a slice into his mouth.

"Good!" continued Grandpa. "Then let's have a ride on that train!"

***

"Be a dear and take this out to Mary would you?" asked Gran, handing Em a cup of after dinner coffee. Glad to get away from clearing up duties, Em padded barefoot across the wooden kitchen floor, out through the French windows, along the terrace and down the wide stone steps into the garden.

It took her several minutes to find Aunt Mary, hidden as she was in a rose arbour at the far end of the garden that overlooked the panoramic beauty of the bay. It had clearly been made for two to be alone and unseen. Unaware of Em's approach, Aunt Mary was evidently miles away, watching the orange orb of the setting sun fall into the purple sea.

"A penny for your thoughts?" asked Em, as her shadow fell across her great aunt and made her look up.

"I was thinking of you, dear" she said, "and your young man." Em was lost for words but it didn't matter as the old lady continued without seeking a response. "When I was only a little older than you are now, I met a boy at the seaside. He was tall and blond and funny. We had a lovely time together that holiday but when it came time for us to leave, I was luckier than you; Jack lived only five miles away on the same bus route.

"We used to go the pictures and ride out on our bicycles and it wasn't long before our mothers started whispering about our getting married. But Jack had to do his National Service first, so off he went into the army. He carved me a loveheart on the oak tree we used to sit under in the park. 'Jack loves Joan'."

"Joan?" Em said quizzically.

"Yes," the old lady smiled thinly, "Joan's my first name. I only started using my second name after Jack died. I was his Joan and no-one else's."

"What happened?" gasped Em. Mary's eyes returned to the darkening sea.

"He volunteered to be a human guinea pig to help find a cure for the common cold." She gulped back a sob. "I wrote him a letter begging him not to do it but it was too late. They said he'd never taken part, that he'd died of pneumonia at the barracks, but we never believed it. Mum and Dad tried to get to the bottom of it but they weren't going to tell us anything. And then came the car crash." She sobbed quietly now. "They killed him. They killed them all."

***

Tiptoeing down the hall at 2 a.m. en route to the loo, Anna noticed a light still burning in Em's room. Poking her head round the door, she saw her daughter sitting by the window, wrapped in a blanket, staring out across the moonlit waves. Turning to see who'd opened the door, Em half whispered in a low, sad voice:

"Why didn't you tell me about Aunt Mary?" A look of comprehension passed across Anna's face. She thought for a moment and came to sit beside Em and put an arm around her.

"It's hard to know when to talk about such sad things," she sighed. "She lost her parents very young, but then, of course, so did your Grandpa. But he's always had Grandma to lean on. For Mary it's been much harder. She lost the only two men she ever loved."

"It's just so sad," sniffed Em. Anna hugged her. "So who was the other man? What happened to him?"

"I don't know all the details," Mum continued. "Grandma and Grandpa don't like to talk about it and it's always been understood that we don't upset Aunt Mary by asking questions. All I know is that he was a doctor and somehow roses were involved."

"Roses?" asked Em. Anna looked out into the darkness.

"I remember when I was a child, Grandpa bought Grandma a dozen red roses for her birthday but when Mary came in and saw them in a vase on the dining room table, she went berserk and hurled the vase against the wall. I think she must have gone away for a bit after that because I remember a neighbour helping Grandpa dig up all the rose bushes in the front garden before she came back.

"There's never been a rose in their house to this day."

***

The last few days of the holiday evaporated like summer rain. As they pushed the pile of post back from behind the front door of their All Cannings home, the musty smell made them feel like they'd been away for a month.

The landscape had changed too. Where once had been expanses of waving wheat, the combine harvesters and hay-balers had left combed fields of stubble punctuated by pyramids of cylindrical bales. Summer was nearly over.

CHAPTER 7
BACK TO NORMAL?

In the same way that Em and Joe had been in total denial about coming to live in the countryside, so they had given no thought whatsoever to what lay ahead in September. So when Mum sat up straight and clapped her hands together at the end of breakfast one morning, as she usually did when she had something important to say, they were surprised to hear her talk about it.

"Right then!" she said, "It's been a lovely long summer but it's high time things got back to normal around here. Kim, we can't go on living on our savings, so it's time you started looking for some work."

"Tough break, Dad!" sniggered Joe.

"And you, young man," Mum addressed Joe, "will be going to school."

"No way?" squealed Joe.

"Not laughing now, I see," observed Dad, smirking.

"But what about this home education thing you were talking about?" said Em.

"No longer necessary!" smiled Mum. "I had a last minute ring round of the local schools yesterday and it so happens two pupils in your year have had to move away suddenly so there's room for you after all."

"Oh brilliant," said Joe flatly. "Life just gets better and better."

***

So, on the following Tuesday, Em and Joe stood in the street alongside a number of other kids from the village that they'd seen but didn't know, waiting for the bus to arrive.

Em thought, not for the first time, how glad she was to have Joe and not to have to face a new school on her own. There was something so powerful about having a mirror image of yourself, almost a second you, to stand at your side and face life's challenges with you. She smiled to herself and turned to look at him.

Joe was clearly thinking that he must find a way to talk to the blonde girl with all the black eye make-up. Em made a mental note to try to find out what she was like and point her in Joe's direction if she was nice.

As the bus arrived, a tired old city bus that had had a decidedly patchy new coat of paint to transform it into school transport, Em was relieved to see that most of the seats were full, avoiding the dilemma of where to sit. Too far back could make it look as if you were trying to look hard, too far forward and people might think you were a teacher's pet.

Joe, as usual, charged in headlong, clearing a path to a couple of free seats near the middle. Em followed gratefully in his wake.

As she had expected, almost everyone looked but no-one spoke to them, being too busy catching up with their friends' news after the long holidays.

"So what do we do when we get there?" asked Joe, who always left Em to listen when Mum was telling them such details.

"We go the secretary's office and she'll point us in the right direction," Em replied.

"So, are we in the same class then?" said Joe.

"S'pose so. I know we weren't before but I really think I'd prefer it this time," Em confessed.

"I don't blame you," whispered Joe, "I get the feeling we're the only ones around here who don't own a dog, a horse or a shotgun."

"Actually, I was just thinking how normal everyone looks," smiled Em.

"Don't you remember what Dad said?" grinned Joe. "'They're probably all devil-worshippers and wife-swappers around here.'"

"One: yuk!," replied Em, " two: keep your voice down and, three: he was joking, you idiot!"

"Oh, right," shrugged Joe. "Y'know it's getting to the point now where I can't tell if he's joking or not."

***

The twins first day turned out to be surprisingly pleasant. The school secretary was a large, jolly lady who greeted them like long-lost relatives, asking them where they were from and saying how hard it must be to start a new school at their age. Their form teacher, Mr Davis who, it turned out, was also their Biology teacher, was tall and smiley and keen to just let them find their own feet, as he put it. After introducing them to the class, Em and Joe sat at the only pair of empty tables, right in the centre of the room.

71

As usual, Em noted down all the information the form teacher was giving them while Joe looked around the room until it was time to head for their first lesson. On the way Joe whispered:

"Why does everyone keep smiling at us like that? It's creeping me out!"

"Because they're friendly?" suggested Em. "We're not in London any more. People are just more relaxed down here. So you can stop checking your flies. They're not open!"

***

When they sat down to dinner with the rest of the family that evening they were feeling pretty good.

"So how was school?" asked Dad, as he always did. He was surprised not to get the usual grunts.

"It was all right," conceded Joe. The clang of the saucepan lid Mum dropped on the draining board made them all jump. From Joe this was a major compliment.

"Really?" she said excitedly.

"I don't know if it's just because we're something new or whatever," answered Em, "but everyone was really friendly. Even the older kids."

"I wouldn't get too excited," Joe grinned. "They're probably just softening us up before they sacrifice us."

***

The day had not been so successful for Kim. A ring-round of all his old contacts had brought in nothing but an offer to write a business magazine article on industrial injuries, which he took as a last resort.

72

"The problem is, Kim," one of his old editor friends had said, "you haven't made a name for yourself writing for newspapers or mass market magazines. Try to come up with something funny or quirky and I'll help you sell it in. If you can do that, things would be a lot easier."

After lunch he took a long walk along one of the many footpaths that led away from the village, pushing J asleep in his three wheel all-terrain pushchair. As he walked, Kim replayed the conversation over and over in his mind: "Something funny or quirky", as he walked past fields of cows and waving corn. Coming to the next village along the valley, Kim absentmindedly noted its name before heading back. It wasn't until he was pushing J back across the stable yard that he began to smile broadly to himself.

***

The mystery of why everyone at school was being so nice to the twins was solved at the end of the third week. It turned out that the two empty places in their class had been vacated by the "ASBO Brothers", a pair of thugs who had terrorised everyone, including the teachers, for two whole years, before their parents had finally been evicted from their council house and they'd been forced to move away.

"Sort of makes you feel you have something to live up to," laughed Joe when Em told him.

"No thanks!" said Em. "After all the hassle we had last year with Dad ill and all the problems Mum had with J, I'd like to try and catch up."

"Suit yourself!" shrugged Joe. "So what've we got next?"

"Geography," said Em, and in walked Mr Hemp in his trademark battered brown cords and sandals with socks, by way of confirmation.

"OK kids?" he smiled.

Mr Hemp, Em thought, was one of those people you pitied but couldn't help laughing at. He clearly wanted to be "best mates" with the kids but failed miserably. He was actually quite a nice bloke, but he had a lisp and one of those desperately unsuccessful attempts to grow a beard, presumably to make him look more like a grown-up, that made him an all too easy target. Even Dad, once he'd met him at Parents' Evening, took a pop at him, saying he looked like a sad old hippy who knitted his own breakfast, whatever that meant.

"OK, right, settle down!" began Hemp, feebly. "I thought we'd try something a little different today, hence all this kit from the science labs. You'll remember from our last lesson ..."

"No!" interrupted Bins, a seven-year-old brain in a smelly man's body, from the back row.

"Thank you, Bins. Not had your medication this morning, dear?" hit back Hemp, raising a few sniggers and an "Ooh!" from the class. But Hemp knew he was safe. Bins wasn't one for smart come-backs and just went back to picking his nose.

"In our last lesson we were talking about microclimates. Well, it just so happens that we have one right here on our doorstep." And at this, he pulled the dust sheet off the large object lying on the front bench and motioned the children to gather round. "This is a scale model of the Pewsey Vale I've borrowed from the headmaster's office, so hands off! It is also, as I hope you will remember from the lesson on glaciation, a perfect example of a U-shaped valley.

"Now in here," he pointed towards what looked like a large, metal thermos, "is dry ice. That's frozen carbon dioxide. If you touch this, your hands *will* come off!" He unclipped the lid and a billow of white smoke puffed out of the container's neck.

"So, if I take a small piece of this and pop it into the model, you will see that the valley fills with one big cloud. Very *Hound of the Baskervilles*!"

"Wot?" It was Bins again.

"Sherlock Holmes? Big dog? Oh, forget it!" sighed Hemp. "You can see that the cloud, which in this instance represents the atmosphere, just sits in the valley, trapped by its high sides. And even if I take this hairdryer and blow some wind across the top of the valley, the atmosphere just circulates and is contained by the two sets of hills."

CHAPTER 8
THE CHEESE KNIFE OF DAMOCLES

It was no surprise to Em that, after the first month or so at their new school, she was still struggling to really make friends, or so it seemed to her, and Joe had made loads, mainly through the universal language of all boys: football.

Joe's new best mate was a particularly tall boy with a shock of red hair and freckles who everyone called Mickey. This wasn't his real name (which he hated and had never told anyone) but as his surname was Finn he'd picked up the nickname at primary school and it had stuck. As it turned out, Mickey lived a mile or so along the canal path at Honeystreet, a short line of houses, a pub and a sawmill just below the White Horse, so he'd often come over to play football with Joe and some of the other lads he knew in All Cannings.

Em had often wondered what it would be like to be popular and looked at the thinner, girlier, more perfect-looking girls, who were always in a group together, and wondered why it was she cared. She had good friends back in London, who she texted and emailed regularly, and she knew she'd see them again, but it didn't stop her feeling lonely.

That said, she had been adopted by a group of what Mum would have called "alternative thinkers", a half a dozen boys and girls who mainly wore black, skateboarded a lot and would rather die than listen to anything that was in the Top 40. With no-one else really making an effort to get to know her, Em was glad to have someone to hang out with. Why they wanted to hang out with her she didn't know, and didn't much care.

It was hard to figure out who, if any of them, was the "leader", which pleased Em. Jez was the tallest but by far the quietest, while Nic was the cheekiest (and the cutest), and Tim the poshest and the brainiest. Of the three girls, Tam was the smiley one, Clare the angry feminist, and Jess so white she was almost blue.

***

And so it was, on the morning of the French field trip into Devizes to talk to a delegation from its twin town in the Loire, Em and Joe found themselves stepping down from the school bus into the Market Square.

"Alors, tout le monde en ligne s'il vous plaît!" cried Madame Jones, the French mistress, much to the amusement of several passers-by.

"Does she *have* to do that?" Em asked Tam as they all cringed.

"Never misses a chance to show off, that one," growled Clare.

As they stood in line, waiting for the rest of the group to join them, Em noticed that there was also a French market underway in the square. Rows of stalls decked out with red, white and blue bunting selling, and smelling of, salamis, smoked garlic, crepes, croissants and baguettes, all to the inevitable cheesy accordion music.

"Cheese!" said Joe.

"You're telling me," smiled Em.

"No," he caught Em's arm, "*Cheese!*"

Following the line of his darting glance, as he desperately tried not to let anyone else notice, Em slowly turned and instantly wished the ground would swallow her up.

There, not ten metres away, dressed in a stripy blue and white jersey, with a string of onions around his neck, a beret on his head and a huge, fake moustache under his nose, stood their father. He was presiding over a stall groaning with cheeses under a huge banner with the words "*Les Fromages de Stanton Saint Bernard*" on it.

"Oh ... my ... God!" said Em involuntarily, raising her hands to cover her face.

"What's wrong?" asked Nic, instantly twigging there was something here he could work with.

"Oh, nothing, nothing. I've never seen a French market before, that's all," Em back-tracked feebly.

"Oh yeah, right!" said Nic doubtfully, staring in all directions. "Like I'd believe that! What did you see, an old boyfriend or something?"

"Yeah, that's it," said Em a little too quickly, "I thought I saw someone I knew but I was wrong." And at that moment, to her immense relief, they were led off to the Town Hall.

***

"I'm not joking Mum, I thought I was going to *die*!" squealed Em that evening when they got home. "I have never been so embarrassed in all my life. If anyone ever finds out about this, I swear I'm never setting foot in that school again!"

"Oh, come on Em," reasoned Mum, "it couldn't have been that bad."

"Not that *bad*!" Em almost screamed. "HE HAD A BIKE AND HE WAS WEARING A BERET! HOW *BAD* COULD IT BE?"

"All right! Calm down," laughed Dad.

"Don't you 'calm down' me," stormed Em, "I'm not talking to you until you promise never, and I mean NEVER, to do anything like that again."

"OK, look I'm sorry," said Dad. "Let's sit down and I'll tell you what this is all about."

Em slowly took a seat and sat rigidly cross-armed, at the kitchen table. "I told you I was having trouble getting work, so I spoke to a few friends and they advised me to come up with something different and quirky to write an article about. Well, when we met Sally and her family on holiday, she told Mum about all the practical jokes we used to play in college and I thought, why not?

"Anyway, I met a dairy farmer from one of the farms over in Stanton St Bernard and when I told him what I had in mind, he thought it was a brilliant idea, as long as he got to keep all the profits."

"So?" asked Em, flatly.

"So," continued Dad, "I've already managed to sell the article to five magazines and, now I have the photos, I'm hoping to interest a whole lot more."

"He has photos," groaned Joe.

"We're dead!" said Em, desperately. "Do you realise this is going to hang over us for years? We'll get pelted with cheese triangles! I mean, if they serve macaroni cheese for lunch, we might as well just take the rest of the week off."

"It's all right," said Dad, "I haven't used my real name. If I want to do more of these, I can't have people knowing who I am."

"He's going to do more," Joe groaned.

"Oh come on!" interrupted Mum. "No one knows who your Dad is around here. They'll never find out."

"Oh right!" snorted Joe. "You know what a blabbermouth he is. I bet half the pubs in the area know all about it!"

"I *am* still sitting here you know," said Dad petulantly, "and for your information I was extremely discreet. No-one knows apart from the farmer and he's sworn to secrecy or I demand the profits back."

"And look on the bright side," added Mum. "Your Dad may be an embarrassment but this way we get to eat!"

***

Sitting in Biology the following Monday, Em and Joe were still expecting a shower of grated parmesan or a blob of camembert to fly in their direction with a selection of lousy jokes, but none came. Perhaps Mum was right and everyone's Dad was as embarrassing as theirs.

"Just wait 'til all the magazines come out," muttered Joe pessimistically.

"Let it go," mumbled Em. "If it happens, it happens."

"Want to share your thoughts with the rest of the class, you two?" asked Mr Davis suddenly.

"Er, no, sorry," said Em apologetically.

"Good. Well if you'd care to listen in to this next bit," the teacher added pointedly, "you might find it useful in next week's test!" There were several groans from around the classroom.

"So, as I was saying before I so rudely interrupted myself, the word 'poxy' that some of you delight in using, actually derives from an often deadly skin disease, called smallpox, that left its victims horribly scarred. The reason we no longer hear of this disease today is that 200 years ago, up the road from here in Gloucestershire, lived a country doctor called Edward Jenner.

"Now he had heard an old wives' tale that milkmaids never caught the disease and decided to investigate. What he discovered was that those working with cows often caught cowpox, a similar but much less dangerous skin disease.

"And so (and this is the good bit!), he decided to experiment on a little boy by first injecting him with the pus from the spots of a sufferer of cowpox," there was a hail of comments of "Yuk!" and "Gross!" from all sides of the room, "and then injecting him with deadly smallpox!

"The boy initially fell ill but soon recovered, thus proving Jenner's theory that a lesser dose of a less

81

deadly version of a virus stimulates the body's defences enough to fight off the more fatal variants. In a word, he had invented the vaccine."

CHAPTER 9
HALLOWEEN

Given Em's belief that she had basically faded into the background at school, she was stunned when Jane, the prettiest of the popular group of girly girls approached her one lunchtime.

"Hi Em!" she smiled sweetly. "I was wondering if you'd like to come to my party on Halloween. It's fancy dress. Here's the details."

"Oh, er, thanks!" Em just managed to blurt out before Jane had swung round, her long blonde hair trailing as if in a shampoo commercial.

"Oh, and bring your brother," Jane added as she walked away across the playground. "I think he's really cute!"

"What was that about?" asked Clare, crossing to meet Em.

"She invited me to her party."

"Oh no, not another one!" Clare grimaced.

"Sorry?" asked Em.

"She's been doing this every year since primary school," explained Clare. "Her dad's the biggest property developer around here, so every year she gets to throw a big party, which she tries to make out is all exclusive, but we all end up getting invited. All so she can spend weeks swanning around asking people to come and then her parents get to show off their enormous house."

Em smiled. "And how enormous is it?"

"Well, let's just say that judging by the size of the towers, her Dad's trying to compensate for something."

***

Clare's predictions proved correct down to the very smallest detail and so Halloween found Em sitting in an eight-seater taxi with Joe, Jez, Nic, Tim, Tam, Clare and Jess – doing a passable impression of The Addams Family – on the way to Jane's party.

"Every year we say we won't go just to spite her but every year the chance to be ignored by everyone else outside school as well is just too great for us to resist," grinned Nic.

"Don't forget the booze," added Tim.

"Or all those tanked up girls," returned Nic.

"So pathetic!" said Clare in disgust.

"Well, at least we didn't throw up in their birdbath last year," sneered Tim.

"You swore you'd never mention that!" snapped Clare.

"Oh come on you guys!" laughed Tam in her usual cheery voice, "it'll be fun. I can't wait to see what everyone's wearing."

"Well if they look any more convincing than Jess I'll eat her pointy hat," sniggered Joe.

"It's Jessika with a K if you don't mind," she said in her usual light and thin voice. "I've decided to become a pagan."

"Oh?" said Jez. Which was the most he ever seemed to say. This did, however, generate the impression that he was a very good listener.

"Yes," Jess continued, "I want to feel more at one with nature and the mystical forces that flow through the landscape."

The car fell silent. No-one could think of a single thing to say.

***

The house, when they saw it, was simply stunning.

"Well, it's certainly different," was the best Em could muster once the taxi had dropped them in the driveway.

"You can't buy taste," added Tim, sniffily.

"A pink brick house with white columns and towers at each corner," said Joe sarcastically. "You've got to admit it's brave."

"It's even better inside!" said Clare, pulling Em by the arm towards the front door which was flanked for the occasion by a pair of illuminated, grinning plastic pumpkins.

"Classy!" noted Nic "But not a patch on the concrete statues on the front lawn."

No sooner had Tam reached out to push the doorbell than there was a loud crack of thunder and the door swung open to reveal Count Dracula.

Normally Em would have been terrified by something like this. Truth be told, she was still scared of the dark and the recent nightmares hadn't helped alleviate this primal fear, but this particular Dracula was another thing altogether. Five foot four, bald and fat, the only thing scary about him was his nasal hair.

85

"Evening Mr. Smith," chorused Jez, Nic, Tim, Tam, Clare and Jess.

"Did ah scare you? Did ah?" said the Count in a squeaky voice. "Ah got the thunder effect off 't Internet. Dead good, i'nt it!"

"Stop blathering and lerrum in, Gerald!" came a woman's strong Yorkshire accent from somewhere behind him, and as they trooped into the hallway they saw its source, a perfectly passable Cruella DeVille.

"Hello, Mrs Smith," they chorused again, and the formalities over with, they awkwardly sidled into the enormous reception room where about a hundred people of varying ages and in an array of outlandish costumes were already making light work of the buffet. It looked like a wedding in hell.

A tall figure in a skeleton costume approached.

"All right, Joe!"

"Mickey?"

"Yeah, come on, pile in, the food's great!"

Em had to admit that, despite the others' carping, Jane's parents certainly knew how to throw a party. How often do you see party sausages that look like fingers, boiled eggs coloured to look like eyeballs, punch with the consistency of blood and glowing green jelly? The atmosphere was good too, no doubt helped along by whatever the "blood" was spiked with, as well as the fact that most people couldn't really tell who they were dancing with.

After one particularly long spell on the makeshift dance floor with the other girls, Em noticed Joe had been cornered by Jane, who, for reasons known only to herself, seemed to have come as Princess Barbie.

"Why's she dressed like that?" Em asked Clare.

86

"She says she's a white witch," said Clare. "So she's half right!" she added, giggling.

"She always needs to be the centre of attention," chipped in Jess.

"I see she's got her hooks into your brother, then," noted Clare.

"He can look after himself," Em reassured them, hoping she was right.

Just then she noticed that though Joe was being talked to by what was widely acknowledged to be the prettiest girl in the school, he wasn't looking at her. His eyes were fixed on the hallway, where a redheaded girl in a blood red top, black miniskirt and red fishnet tights had made a late entrance. Em instantly recognised the girl from the Science Museum.

"Oh dear!" said Em with mock sympathy. "I don't think Jane's going to have things all her own way."

"Hey!" said Nic coming out of the crowd. "We've found something interesting in the snooker room!" Em looked doubtfully at Clare. "Oh, come on! Come on!" Nic insisted, looping his arms through theirs and steering them towards a door.

***

Mr Smith's snooker room, resplendent with zebra-print sofas, was dark except for a low-hanging, shaded light over the snooker table. In its centre, in a pool of light was a board with a glass on it.

"What do you think of that?" said Nic triumphantly.

"What is it?" asked Tam.

"It's a Ouija board," said Jess. "It's supposed to be a link to the spirit world. There's 'Yes' and 'No' and the letters are used to spell out words."

"Whose is it?" asked Em.

"Who cares?" smiled Nic. "Who wants a go?"

"Count me out," said Em, backing away to settle on the arm of one of the sofas.

"Suit yourself," said Nic. "What about you guys? Scared too?"

A combination of Nic's provocation, the alcohol and the party atmosphere was enough to ensure the others soon surrounded the board.

"So what do we do, then?" asked Tam. "Hold hands?"

"That's a séance," said Tim condescendingly. "With a Ouija board we all put one finger on the glass." They all leant forward and did as he said.

Nothing happened.

"Now what?" said Clare fixing Nic with an impatient stare.

"I thought it was supposed to start moving around and answer our questions," he said doubtfully.

"Perhaps we should ask one then?" said Tam, though the tone of her voice gave the slight impression that she'd prefer if they didn't.

"Any ideas?" said Nic looking around at a row of blank faces.

"Are there any messages for anyone here?" said Jez, so unexpectedly that the others jumped.

"Damn, Jez!" said Clare. "If you're going to start talking all of sudden, could you at least warn us first?"

"That's completely illogical," noted Tim, "I mean if Jez had to warn us first he'd still have to say something." But before Clare could react, they all noticed the movement.

It was infinitesimal at first. More like a vibration. Nic was just about to make a crack about it being a passing truck when the glass lurched towards the "YES".

The fear and excitement was palpable.

"Who's it for?" said Tam in a hoarse whisper, looking around at the others. Before anyone could answer, the glass moved again.

"M…A…R…Y," read Tim. "Who's Mary?" Em felt a blast of cold shoot up her body and her blood began to sing in her ears. She opened her mouth to speak but couldn't.

"What's the message?" said Nic with a tremor in his voice.

"P…E…A…C…E…" read Tim.

"Well at least that's positive," said Tam, with a slight sigh of relief.

"There's more!" whispered Jess urgently.

"W…I…L…L…," continued Tim, "S…O…O…N… B…E… T…H…I…N…E."

Em had stood up and was backing silently towards the door, her head pounding, unable to breathe. Suddenly the door flew open and she swung round to see the reflected flash of light from a scythe that instantly blinded her. Stumbling backwards into the room, her arms instinctively raised in defence, she screamed and fainted.

***

Em came to in a bedroom on a pile of coats with Tam and Jess splashing water on her face and the others crowded round looking concerned. Nic looked extremely guilty. At first Em was hit by a wave of panic as she had no idea who these people were or where she was. Her darting eyes eventually rested on Joe and she felt a sudden sense of relief.

"What have these idiots been doing to you?" he said, helping her to sit up.

"It wasn't *our* fault ..." began Nic.

"No, it was *your* fault," snapped Clare, ending Nic's sentence for him.

"You can't blame me for the Grim Reaper," Nic tried again. Em made an instinctively fearful grab for Joe's arm.

"Would you shut up!" said Clare angrily. "She's scared witless."

"What are you on about?" Joe asked Nic.

"Some jerk dressed as the Grim Reaper, with a skeleton face mask, a metal scythe, the whole lot, burst in looking for the loo and frightened the life out of Em."

"That's not all, is it Nic?" added Jess.

"Well, no," admitted Nic, "we were playing with a Ouija board. But Em wasn't taking part or anything and the message was for someone called Mary so I don't see what ..."

"That's her name," interrupted Joe, flatly. "Em is short for Mary."

***

The next day, Sunday, Em stayed in bed all day. Not having dared to sleep, she had sat with all the lights on, watching television on its lowest volume setting, as far away from the window as she could get. As the sun finally rose, she crawled into bed and succumbed to the warm wave of fatigue.

Joe did his best to cover for Em, saying she'd caught a chill.

"It's all right, Joe," Dad smirked. "She can sleep off her hangover in peace."

***

Monday at school was odd. Having slept for most of the preceding 24 hours, Em felt like she had returned, refreshed, from a long weekend away, the drama of Saturday night a weird and distant memory.

Her mates were all looking extremely concerned as she arrived in class.

"Are you OK?" asked Tam, hugging her.

"I'm fine," said Em, truthfully. "Just a bit embarrassed."

"What, about being called *Mary*?" smirked Nic.

"Like you can talk, *Dominic*," said Clare.

"Dominic?" laughed Tim, "Is that your name?"

"Yeah, so what *Timothy*?" said Nic grumpily. "I don't see that you and *Tamara* have got much room to talk."

"Leave Tam alone," insisted Jez.

"Ooh, the beast awakes!" mocked Nic. "Just what is Jez short for, I wonder. Jesmond? Jeremiah? Jehosephat?"

Just as it seemed Jez was going to lose his cool for the first time in his life and land one on Nic, Mr Davis walked in.

***

"Oh, hello you two," said Dad as Em and Joe arrived home and walked across the stable yard. "Come into the storeroom for a minute. I've just unpacked a little something for you."

The storeroom, yet another old stable, was unusually dark with just the dull, early November daylight struggling through the door to illuminate the usual detritus of family life. In the centre of the room on a big box stood an oblong of black plastic with chrome detail and a clear plastic cover. "Remember this? It's my old record player."

"And why would we want that?" asked Joe dubiously.

"Well, word has got back to your Mum of your little adventure with the Ouija board the other night," Em reddened, "and I thought I'd show you what we used to do when I was a lad."

"Oh yeah? What's that then?" said Joe, stepping closer to the box. Em remained silent.

"Let me show you." Dad pulled a black, twelve-inch disc out of a vividly illustrated record sleeve with "Iron Maiden" written on it and placed it on the turntable.

"Er, doesn't that thing need to be plugged in?" said Joe.

"Not necessarily. Now come closer and listen very carefully." He lowered the needle on the record and, with one finger on the label in the middle, began to turn it very slowly in an anticlockwise direction.

At first there were a lot of odd sounds, then a silence and then suddenly a slurred, but nonetheless discernible voice.

"Dooown't mess with thiiiings you doooon't understaaaand."

There was a brief moment while Joe and Em took in the words.

"Oh, very funny Dad!" said Em, angrily. "I was really scared!" Joe just chuckled.

"Well you ought to be scared," said Dad, and Em was surprised he wasn't laughing but serious and even a bit angry himself.

"It's all very well taking an interest in this stuff," Dad continued, "but you don't want to get to a point where you're willing to believe whatever's served up to you without thinking it through; that's just plain dangerous." He paused. "You both have good brains and brains are for calm reasoning and for getting to the truth."

"And what exactly is 'the truth', Dad?" said Em, flatly.

"The truth?" sighed Kim. "Good question." He thought for a moment. "The truth is a dangerous thing, sometimes even a deadly one. The truth is that even after thousands of years of so-called civilisation the vast majority of people still want to believe only what they want to believe, even if the truth is staring them right in the face. And it's also the truth that these people, when forced to acknowledge reality, can get very upset.

"They want to believe in ghosts and ghouls and spirits, or that a ring of stones, that just happens to line up precisely with the stars, is something mystical, when it's probably just a calendar. Or they want to believe that shapes in a cornfield are messages from outer space. And woe betide anyone who dares contradict them!"

"So are you saying that we shouldn't believe in anything, then?" said Joe.

"Of course I'm not," said Dad. "Quite the opposite, in fact. What I'm saying is that you should believe only those things you can either prove outright or that seem to be the most probable. Everything in this world is the way it is for a sound, logical reason. So, if ancient man dragged thousands of tons of stone across the country to make some monuments, then he had a damn good reason for doing it."

"And," followed on Em, pensively, "I suppose if crop circles started appearing in the middle of a field one day, then there's a perfectly logical explanation for that too."

"Yes," smiled Kim, glad to feel he was getting his point across, "I suppose there must be."

CHAPTER 10
ROUND THE BEND

The following Saturday, the whole family headed into Marlborough for their various reasons. Dad and Joe needed haircuts, Mum and Em wanted to do some clothes shopping and J wanted to hear the clocks go "dong".

After a little bartering, it was agreed that Dad and Joe would go to the barbers first whilst Mum and Em took J to the playground and to see one church clock strike the hour, and then they'd meet up for a coffee so Dad and Joe could take over the baby-minding duties for the rest of the morning.

So, with J straining at his reins, Em and Mum crossed Waitrose's car park and headed for the play area.

"Are you all right, Em?" asked Mum, looping her arm through Em's.

"Yes, why?" Em answered defensively.

"Well, you don't seem very happy at the moment," said Mum, "and I was wondering if there's anything I can do?"

"No, it's nothing really," Em shrugged. "I'm just a bit tired. I'm not sleeping very well at the moment." Mum smiled sympathetically.

"Is everything OK at school? I mean, no-one's being mean to you or anything?"

"No, Mum, nothing like that." Her tone had a finality that Mum recognised from her own teenage years. Em didn't want to talk about it and there was no point trying to push it.

"Oh, well, OK," Mum squeezed Em's arm with hers, "but if you want to talk about anything, I'm always here."

"That's great, Mum, thanks," smiled Em, weakly.

As they got to the playground, surrounded by water meadows in the bottom of the valley, J ran to the merry-go-round and Em followed instinctively.

"Do you want to join him? This used to be your favourite too when you were little," laughed Mum as Em sat on one side with J facing her. Any chance to sit down, Em thought. Mum grabbed the nearest metal handle and heaved the merry-go-round into life.

Em immediately understood she'd made a mistake. With her head already spinning with lack of sleep, she tried to focus on anything static, but all she could see was the blurring of the cars, the scrub grass and the trees. As her head began to swim, she instinctively gripped the bright orange, plastic seat tight, feeling the sharp edge cutting into her hands. Her head flopping forwards, she was able to focus on the textured rubber floor of the merry-go-round and gain some sense of equilibrium. Closing her eyes and feeling her brains flop about like a raw egg inside its shell, she prayed for it to stop.

"Slide!" ordered J, and Em felt Mum mercifully slowing them down. She opened her eyes to see J wobbling off to the next bit of play equipment.

"Er, Mum," said Em shakily, "do you mind if I go on to the café now?"

"No, of course not, darling," smiled Mum, handing her some money. "Here. Can you order me a latte and J an apple juice? Have something to eat. It'll do you good to get some sugar in your veins."

Em re-crossed the little bridge over the so-called River Kennet, which looked no more than a long, narrow duck pond at this point, and then turned down the ramp to the Mustard Seed Café.

It was a funny little place, Em had thought the first time she saw it. What had presumably once been a very small, two storey house close by the water was now stranded between two large car parks. Once you were inside, however, and occupying a table by the floor to ceiling windows onto the river and the water meadows beyond, it was easy to forget the hustle and bustle of shoppers outside.

The other odd thing about the café was that it was in large part also a Christian book shop, something they all studiously ignored as the homemade cakes, especially the lemon drizzle cake, were superb. Em was glad to be alone as she made her order at the counter, as she was in no mood to tolerate Dad's usual excruciating joke about their "heavenly" cakes.

Taking a corner place by the window, Em looked down into the water and followed the widening ripples across the surface made by a solitary duck bobbing. It was a mercifully short wait until her second breakfast arrived.

***

The rest of the morning seemed a blur to Em. After the café, she decided to tag along with Dad and Joe as they took J to see the white church clock strike 11. After a slow trawl around the various stalls in the market and a visit to Ducks toyshop to find J a toy tractor, they met up with Mum and headed home for lunch.

At the end of the meal, Dad leant back in his chair, and looked curiously at the twins.

"Decidedly pasty complexions," he mused. "Never mind, we know how to change that!"

"We thought it might be nice to go for a family walk," explained Mum "like we said we would when we moved to the country." Joe pulled a face and gave Em a quick sideways glance.

"What? Now?" asked Em, dully.

"Yep! It's a beautiful sunny day, so let's not waste it. Come on! All into the car for the Priest family mystery tour! Chop, chop!" said Dad, leaping to his feet and shepherding his reluctant progeny to the door.

***

A brief ride brought them to a roundabout crossing the A4 and then over a rise and ...

"Woah! What's that thing?" cried Joe from the back seat. Over to their right, about a quarter of a mile away, stood an enormous grass-covered hill that most closely resembled a cross between a huge steamed pudding and a traffic cone.

"That's Silbury Hill!" said Mum, evidently satisfied at Joe's reaction.

"How big is it?" asked Em, leaning forwards to see round Joe and out the window.

"About 40 metres tall and about 200 round, I think," smiled Mum. "Pull in left here, Kim."

They rolled into a small car park and got out.

"Don't you think it looks a lot like the mountain the aliens land on in *Close Encounters*?" asked Dad, and was met by a line of blank faces. "You know, the one Richard Dreyfus keeps sculpting out of mashed potato and shaving foam and whatever."

"What *is* he talking about?" Em asked Mum.

"Another one of his 'classic' films, dear," replied Mum, patting Em's hand in mock reassurance.

"So what's it for then?" asked Em.

"Probably a burial chamber," suggested Dad. "Sort of an ancient English version of a pharaoh's pyramid."

"Not that they've ever actually found a burial chamber in it," added Mum. "There are some big mounds – barrows they call them – that were definitely used for important burials, over in that direction by East and West Kennet, though."

"So do we have to walk all the way over there, then?" said Joe, pointing at the distant monument.

"Oh no," said Mum, "that's just by the bye. We're going this way!" and she pointed towards a path in the far corner of the car park.

The two information boards they soon passed quickly gave away what they had been brought to see.

"Oh, this is Avebury!" said Em, excited despite her fatigue. "Do you remember I told you about it, Joe? The stone circles?"

"Uh huh," grunted Joe. His wholly unimpressed attitude at the idea of stones arranged in a circle changed immediately, however, once they turned the corner. "Wow! It's like a massive half-pipe!" he exclaimed, confronted by the ten-metre deep ditch that surrounded the site.

"Don't think they'd want you skateboarding here, son," laughed Dad.

"Come and look at the stones!" called Mum, marching off ahead with J in her arms.

"Can we actually go inside?" asked Em, who remembered reading that you couldn't at Stonehenge.

"Yep! Come on!"

They walked up a little village street past a line of thatched and slate-roofed houses and passed through a small wooden gate into the first part of the central enclosure. Before them stood a line of weather beaten grey-green stones, some almost two storeys high, arranged in a perfect arc.

"So who made this then? What's it for?" asked Em.

"Two very good questions," replied Mum. "Sadly no-one knows. That's why it's all so mysterious!"

"Do they know how old it is?" asked Dad.

"It said four to five thousand years old on the internet," said Em.

"See!" Mum said to Dad, "I told you they didn't just use the computer for video games!" Dad stuck his tongue out in response.

"How many stones are there?" asked Joe, ignoring his parents' implied insult.

"About 120, I think, arranged in three circles," explained Mum, "one large one around the inside of the ditch, then two smaller separate ones inside that."

They returned to the smaller village road and crossed over to the little chapel that doubled up as the local tourist information office and spent a few minutes leafing through the various leaflets and selecting a few to take home.

"Do you guys fancy a little walk round while I take a look in the antique shop?" hinted Mum as they left the chapel. With weary nods, Dad and the twins headed back across the road with J, past the various picnic tables outside The Red Lion pub.

"Afternoon," said Dad suddenly, to a man sitting, reading a newspaper at one of them, the twins looking round just in time to see Mr Hemp raise a quick hand in acknowledgement. "Really weird when you see school teachers out of school, isn't it?" chuckled Dad. "You always assume the caretaker stuffs them all in a dusty cupboard on Friday night before pulling them all out again on Monday morning. Especially ones like him!"

They followed the signs to the museums (there were two), the shop and the café, all arranged around an old farmyard in front of Avebury Manor.

"House! Circle!" cried J, running towards the dovecote in the centre of the yard.

"Very good J!" said Em, picking him up. What else can you see that's a circle?"

"Ball!" said J, pointing to a sculpted stone detail over the gateway to the manor house.

"And what's that on the end of the building?" asked Em.

"Clock!" squealed J in delight.

"And what do clocks do?" asked Em.

"Bong!" bonged J, giggling.

***

As they passed through the church's lych-gate back onto the village road, they found they'd come full circle back to the end of the car park path. Looking back up the road towards the pub, they noticed Mum hurrying towards them.

"Kim!" she said anxiously "I think I've just seen that so-called policeman who came to see us!"

"Really?" asked Dad. "Where?"

"Just outside the pub," Mum replied. "He was on a motorbike and he had a helmet on so I could only see part of his face but I saw his eyes. I'm sure it's him."

"Well come on then," said Em, "what are we waiting for?"

They all ran up the street as fast as they could, Dad puffing along with J in his arms. As he finally caught up to the others beside the road junction he asked between deep breaths:

"Well?"

"He's gone," said Mum dejectedly.

"Damn!" exclaimed Dad. And then, after a pause, "What about that teacher? Why don't we ask him if he saw anything?"

Em, Joe and Kim looked back across the pub car park to see the table now empty except for the open newspaper, a hardly touched pint of beer and a still smouldering cigarette in the ashtray.

"Maybe he's popped inside for a moment," suggested Mum.

"I don't think so," said Joe, looking around. "His car's gone as well."

***

The atmosphere in the house that evening was a little unsettled. Once the kids had gone to bed, Kim tried to make light of Anna's concerns that this "policeman" might be following them.

"He's probably after me for impersonating a French farmer," grinned Kim. "It's probably illegal under some EU ruling. They're most likely blockading the ports as we speak!

"And talking of crimes, how unbelievably British is it to have a pub, an antiques shop and a main road running straight through a World Heritage Site? That information board compared the place to the Taj Mahal. I bet they haven't got a pub tacked on the side of that!"

"Oh, do be serious, Kim!" chided Anna.

"What is there to be serious about?" shrugged Kim. "You think you recognised some bloke wearing a full set of motorbike leathers and a crash helmet. None of us got a good look at him so, to be honest, I think it was probably someone who just happened to look a bit like him."

"Well, OK," Anna said doubtfully, "if you say so. But I was so sure it was him."

***

When Em's head finally hit the pillow, she was convinced she would sleep for a week. Her drop into deep slumber was so instantaneous that when she woke suddenly three hours later, her cold shoulder confirmed that she was still in the same position. Pulling the duvet up and rolling over she dropped again into deep sleep but this time everything seemed animated, an amalgam of sleep and consciousness, a multicolour light show of her imagination's creation.

She saw herself falling into sleep like a pebble into a dark pool, the expanding ripples first creating intricate yellow circles of flattened corn, then grassy fields of stone circles and then the chalk white head of the Angel that began to rotate faster and faster until she was back, gripping the merry-go-round seat and staring at the textured floor as the world blurred around her.

She flipped her head back up and her surroundings changed again. She was at Avebury now, floating above it this time, but somehow the landscape had changed: the road, the pub and the houses were nowhere to be seen.

A dense white mist seeped from the ground and slowly swirled like the dry ice in Hemp's experiment.

"Circle!" she heard J cry repeatedly. "Circle! Circle! Circle!" as she looked down to see first the stones, then the clock, the dovecote, the sculpted ball and the top of Silbury Hill, slowly rotating.

There was a crack of thunder and a bolt of lightning arced across the landscape like the Reaper's flashing scythe.

"Circle!" said the deep, breathless voice she had come to dread, and the outer ring of stones below her described the cowl of a cloak. "Circle!" and the two inner circles became piercing green eyes.

Another flash of lightning and she recognised the face.

"Peace will soon be thine," the Policeman sighed.

CHAPTER 11
FIELD TRIP

"All right, settle down!" Monday afternoon had come round again and Ms Scott, Em and Joe's English teacher, was calling the class to order.

"Now, as Halloween is still fresh in our memories, it's perhaps only appropriate that we come to Act One, Scene Five of Hamlet, where our hero first encounters the ghost of his father."

"Oooohh!" A ghoulish moan came from the back of the classroom.

"Yes, thank you Bins. Don't forget Parents' Evening is just around the corner, lovey." Bins fell silent and the rest of the class knew why. If you were to write a list of all the reasons you might have for not wanting to be Bins, his dad would always be at the very top.

"Right then, who wants to read today?" Silence. She looked around the room. "Ah, you, the new girl, Em isn't it? You can be Hamlet and Robert, you can be the ghost."

Em's heart sank. Bad enough to have to sit here and try to understand this, worse to look a complete idiot trying to make it sound anything like normal English.

They slowly worked through the scene, Em turning over each page in the copy that Mum had lent them; it was the one Anna had used for her English degree and Em was pleased to see that she'd made lots of useful notes in the margin.

Turning another page, she was confronted by two lines of text underlined in red ink and once Em had spoken them Ms Scott asked her to pause.

"'There are more things in heaven and earth than are dreamt of in your philosophy'," repeated the teacher. "Now what do you suppose that might mean?"

"There's more to this world than meets the eye?" asked Nigel, the squeaky-clean class brainiac in his usual superior tone.

"Hmm! Not bad," conceded Ms Scott. "And what do you think is meant here by 'philosophy'? No, not you again Nigel. Does anyone else have any ideas?"

Em read straight from her mother's margin notes: "A natural philosopher was the old name for a scientist, so 'philosophy' here means science."

"Excellent!" said Ms Scott, with a note of surprise, accompanied by an unhappy snort and a glare from Nigel. Em felt slightly guilty but enjoyed meeting Nigel's look with a wide grin.

"OK," said Ms Scott, "let's open this up to a wider discussion. What sorts of things are there in heaven and earth that go beyond the realm of our knowledge?" Silence. "Oh, come on! We live in Wiltshire! Nigel?"

"Stonehenge," said Nigel smugly.

"Good! Any more?"

"UFOs?" asked the usually silent Stacey.

"Yes, and thank you for joining us." Ms Scott smiled. Stacey reddened.

"What about crop circles?" said Jordan. "No one knows what makes them."

"Yeah! Right!" Joe snorted.

"No, they're real!" insisted Jordan. "My Mum swears by them, the real ones that is, not the ones made by drunk students. Anyway what do you townies know?"

"All right, keep it friendly, please," intervened Ms Scott. "Anyway, this subject brings me neatly on to your coursework for the rest of this term." Groans. "The subject is Myths, Legends and Folklore. I want you all to pick a theme and let me know what it is by next week."

As the bell rang and they filed out into the hallway, Em caught Joe's eye. "Got any ideas?"

"Yeah," said Joe, "what about an exposé of crop circles for our friend Jordan?"

"Well if you're gonna do that," said Mickey, eavesdropping "I'd ask Hemp. My Dad says 'e was one o' the first to really get into 'em round 'ere."

***

Two minutes later, Em and Joe were standing outside Mr Hemp's classroom waiting for the last pupil to leave. They walked up to his desk and he looked up at them quizzically.

"Oh, hello you two," he smiled "Anything I can help you with?"

"Yes, sir," Em smiled back. "We were wondering if you could tell us what you know about crop circles?"

Looking back on it, Em and Joe agreed it was the most complete and instant change in someone they had ever experienced. Leaping to his feet, his face flushed bright red, veins bulging in his neck, he hissed at them:

"Who put you up to this? Answer me, you little animals? Who?" Em and Joe swayed back in shock and stood rigid in stunned silence. "All right don't tell me, but understand this. If either of you dares mention this to me again, it's a month's detention each. Now get out!" And he flung his arm out and pointed to the door.

"I thought you said this was going to be a laugh?" Em asked Joe as they crossed the playground.

"Who says it isn't?" smirked Joe. "If ever I saw a man with something to hide …"

"We certainly touched a raw nerve," agreed Em "For a moment there, I thought he was going to hit us."

"Yeah, more than a bit out of character wouldn't you say?" mulled Joe.

"Anyway, forget Hemp," said Em. "I think we should start at the beginning. Let's try the library."

Half an hour of web searches later and they had a plan.

***

On Saturday morning, to their parents' great surprise, Em and Joe ate their breakfast at 7.30 and were on their way out of the door at 8.

"You do know it's not a school day?" asked Dad sarcastically from behind his newspaper.

"We just fancied a walk. Bye!" said Em, as they hurried out the door, leaving Anna and Kim shrugging at one another.

***

First stop was the field they had identified as being one of the first ever sites of a crop circle.

"Not very impressive, is it?" said Joe, taking a picture of the expanse of rutted mud.

"Can you feel anything?" asked Em.

"Biting cold?" suggested Joe.

"No, I mean really?" asked Em. "According to all that stuff on the web, there's supposed to be an electrical field or some sort of radiation left behind."

"Shame it wasn't an electric radiator. My feet are freezing," said Joe stamping his boots. "Anyway, you can't just feel that stuff, you need a Geiger counter or whatever. Anyway, where are we going next?"

"Well, I thought we might try speaking to some of the locals," said Em looking around a little doubtfully. "We could try that farmhouse?"

"Anywhere that's warmer than here is fine by me," replied Joe, and he started off across the furrowed field.

***

The farmhouse was a bleak affair. Standing in the open plain of the wide valley bottom, it had been battered by the elements for many a long year, most of the recent ones, it seemed, without a new lick of paint to protect it.

Joe, clearly driven by the need to get warm, gave the old door knocker with peeling paint a good workout on the wizened oak door.

"Just a minute!" called out an old voice from behind the door, before a lot of clanking of rusty bolts being drawn back and the clunk as the key turned in the ancient lock.

The door opened a crack and a kindly old man's face appeared.

"Yes?" it asked.

"Hello!" smiled Em in her most appeasing tone. "We're very sorry to bother you but we're doing a school project on the crop circles."

"Oh aah?"

"Er, aah, I mean yes," stumbled Em, "and we wanted to ask you about the one that appeared in your field here," and she pointed.

"Ah, well ee better come in then," grinned the man, throwing wide the door.

The inside of the farm was a perfect match for the exterior, and it's owner was no different. The hunched little old man, in a scrappy old brown cardigan and matching woollen trousers, shuffled in slippers to the seat at the kitchen table nearest to the Aga. Joe and Em leant against it, warming their hands on the rail.

"So yours was one of the first circles to appear, then?" asked Joe, kindly.

"Ah, now let me think," said the old man, stroking his unshaven chin "It were donkey's years ago, mind." He pondered for a moment. "Yes, that would'a bin just before Ma were taken from us."

Oh, I'm sorry," said Joe a little embarrassed.

"They brought 'er back though," grinned the old man.

"I'm sorry?" said Em.

"It were the shoplifting, ya see," explained the old man. "She didn't do it on purpose, mind. She were losing 'er memory and forgot to pay for things. She only died last month."

"Oh, right, sorry," said Joe.

The old man looked up. "You two apologise an awful lot, don't ya? There's nuthin to be sorry for, anyhow. It's just the way o' things. The sun comes up and the sun goes down. One day people come and then one day ..." and he spread his lined, swollen hands.

"So, about the circle ...?" asked Em, trying to get the conversation back on track.

"Well, there's not much to tell, truth be told," shrugged the old man. "One morning I was out walking the fields and there it were. Couldn't make head nor tail of it m'self."

"And did you notice anything strange?" asked Em.

"Well, there were a bluddy great circle in the field!" the old man chuckled. "Can't get much more strange than that!"

"Anything else, I mean?" asked Em patiently.

"Well, yes," conceded the old man. "Next thing we know, we've got all sorts of long-haired types trespassing to get a look at it. Army came and get rid of 'em, though."

"The army?"

"Yeah," smiled the old man. "They were crawling all over round here in them days. Now they mainly fly over, lazy beggars!" He motioned upwards as yet another helicopter flew overhead.

They chatted a little longer, but it was clear there was nothing left to gain from the conversation. Em and Joe reluctantly left the snug confines of the old man's kitchen and stepped back into the cold November air.

111

***

Four more fields, three more freezing hours and a couple of less successful attempts to meet the natives left them with just one useful scrap of information. Standing in All Cannings Community Store to warm up and devour a couple of consolatory bars of Green & Black's Mayan Gold, they fell into conversation with one of the well-spoken ladies behind the counter who suggested that, if they were really interested in finding out about crop circles, they should try The Barge at Honeystreet, the next village beyond Stanton St Bernard.

***

Arriving back at the house as the sun was setting, Em and Joe helped themselves to steaming mugs of tea and a place by the fire. Twenty minutes later Dad tumbled in through the door, weighed down with shopping, Mum having gone off to the Grands for the day with J.

"Dad," asked Em in her sweetest voice, "will you take us to the pub, please?"

"Help me with this and I'll think about it," he grunted, shoving the bags at them. "OK, I've thought about it," he said instantly. "We can go on two conditions: one, no-one tells your Mum."

"Agreed," chorused Em and Joe.

"And, two, you tell me where you've been all day?"

"We were researching our school project," said Em. "Now take us to the pub."

"Not so fast! What school project?"

"I want to prove to this idiot at school that crop circles are a scam," grinned Joe, "so we chose it as the subject of our project on Myths, Legends and Folklore."

"OK, that I can believe," sighed Dad, after a quick pause for reflection. "I didn't think you'd be wasting your weekend to learn anything useful."

"Can we go now?" asked Em impatiently.

"Don't you want to dress up?" asked Dad.

"I don't think it's that sort of a place," said Em.

CHAPTER 12
SILENT RUNNING

"Well, at least it's close by," said Kim, as he came to the T junction beneath the White Horse hill monument at Alton Barnes and took a right towards Honeystreet. The humpback bridge soon loomed up, Em spotting the sign and telling Kim to take the next right.

As they turned into what looked like an enormous timber yard, filled with pallets of wooden stakes and fencing panels, Kim looked doubtfully at Em beside him.

"Are you sure about this?" he asked.

"Keep going," she smiled, using her mother's well-worn expression.

After another 40 metres running alongside the canal and then past a line of houses, the lane opened out to reveal a dilapidated black wooden barn and a large stone building at the water's edge, fronting onto a small beer garden.

"There we are!" announced Em triumphantly.

"OK," said Kim, coming to a stop in the pot-holed car park, "you can have one hour, soft drinks only and I'm coming in for a quick look round first."

As they walked through the dogleg door, their first impressions were of the oppressive dark green and varnished wood décor and the immensely long bar that seemed to dwarf the room. An old black wood burner with an eagle motif sent out a welcoming glow from the hearth.

Em and Kim were surprised to see Joe wave and smile at the barman who welcomed him by name.

"That's Mickey's dad," explained Joe. "Come and say hello." Once the introductions were made and drinks ordered, Em looked around the bar disappointed.

"So what's all this stuff about this being *the* place to come if you're interested in crop circles, then?" she asked.

"Take a look in the back room," indicated Mickey's dad with his head, towards a door from which the distinctive sound of ivory balls connecting was coming.

Popping her head around the door and trying to ignore the four young lads who immediately began staring at her, Em was thrilled to see the walls were covered with crop circle photos and newspaper articles and a map of where they had all appeared.

"Now lie on your back, darlin'" one of the lads laughed dirtily, pointing at the ceiling with his cue. His mates sniggered. Before Em could tell them where to go, she was amazed to see the entire ceiling was an enormous painting depicting crop circles, the stone circles at Avebury and Stonehenge, and the Moon, Sun, Wind and the Green Man.

"Good enough for you?" Mickey's dad asked Em as she came back to find Kim gone and Joe perched on a barstool demolishing his second bag of crisps.

"Yeah, great thanks," smiled Em. "I don't suppose we could come back and take some photos when it's not full of idiots?"

"Yeah, I don't see why not," he replied. "Why the sudden interest?"

"School project," said Joe through his salt and vinegar.

"Oh, fair enough," said Mickey's dad, pulling a pint. "If you're really interested, you should ask some of the 'croppies' who come in. Nuts most of 'em but totally harmless. I would tell you to speak to your Mr Hemp, he was one of the first lot to really show an interest in 'em way back when, but he's been sat in the snug getting hammered since opening time."

"Don't think we'll bother, thank-you," said Joe. "We tried to ask him at school but he threatened us with a month's detention if we even mentioned crop circles to him."

"What?" asked Mickey's dad. "That old dishrag? You're joking!"

"No," admitted Em, "he went bonkers at us."

"Now I really have heard it all," smiled Mickey's dad.

Em slipped off her barstool. "Where did you say he was?"

"Through there," motioned Mickey's dad, "but don't say I didn't warn you."

***

Hemp had indeed crawled inside a bottle. He didn't react as Em and Joe sat at his table, only noticing them as he looked up from the bottom of his latest pint glass.

"Who are you?" he slurred, trying to focus on their faces.

"Em and Joe Priest," Em said.

"Really?" boggled Hemp. "Well if you say so." He squinted at them. "Oh, so you are."

"We wanted to ask you a question," continued Em levelly.

"Ask away, old friend," said Hemp with a drunken grin.

"What's your problem with crop circles?"

"Nothing, I love 'em," he said plainly.

"So why did you threaten us with a month's detention for mentioning them?" Hemp took a gulp and looked jerkily around the room.

"Do you know," he began "I haven't been in here for twenty years. Twenty years! And do you know why?" He leant forward conspiratorially. "Because I was scared."

"Scared of what?" whispered back Em.

"Them."

"Who?"

"Well, I don't know!" he snapped angrily and flopped back in his chair. He thought for a lengthy moment, as if debating with himself. "Oh what does it matter any more?" He leant forward again, his chin so low it was almost resting on his arms. "Twenty years ago, I was just starting out teaching. I used to do a lot of hiking and one morning I found my first crop circle. From then on, it took over my life, and I used to meet up here with all the other croppies and spend many a happy evening drinking and discussing all our outlandish theories about who or what was making the circles and what they might mean. I'd never met so many new friends or felt

117

so happy," he remembered with a drunken, nostalgic smile.

"Until one day," and his face hardened, "I was walking back along the road to the bus stop when a van pulled up alongside me and they dragged me inside." Tears welled up in his eyes.

"All I remember is a lot of very tall men barking orders and hitting me. The rest of it's a blur. I don't remember and, frankly, I don't want to." He took another long gulp.

"Two days later a letter arrived telling me never to come here again or I'd be fitted up as a child molester and lose my job. I panicked, went back to my parents' up north and had them say I was ill. After a while they persuaded me to come back to my flat.

"I looked everywhere for that letter, I wanted them to believe that I hadn't just imagined it all, but it had gone. Vanished!"

"What made you stay here?" asked Em.

"Things were different back then," Hemp said. "If you had a good job, you kept it. And as time went on and nothing happened, I just let myself forget."

"So what are you doing in this pub now?" Joe asked.

"I think I'm going crazy," he smiled crookedly, "I keep seeing things ... people that remind me of what happened," and for the first time since he'd begun talking he took his eyes off them and looked between them out of the window, his head snapping round as he caught sight of someone passing by. The colour drained from his face.

"I've got to go," he said hurriedly, wobbling to his feet. "I've been a fool. For God's sake, forget what I said, all of it!" And he all but ran from the pub, ricocheting off people like a pinball.

"Who was that outside?" Em asked Joe, looking out the window.

"Beats me," said Joe.

"Look!" said Em, her nose now tight against the glass, her eyes straining to see round the corner into the car park. "Who's that getting into that car?"

"What? Where?" asked Joe desperately.

Em slowly leant back and turned to face him. "It's our Policeman!" she said.

***

Once Em and Joe had jostled their way through the mass of bodies in the bottleneck between the oversize bar and the narrow little door, and finally got out into the car park, neither Hemp nor the "policeman" were anywhere to be seen.

"What do we do now?" asked Joe.

"We've got to find Hemp," said Em firmly. "He clearly knows who that other guy is and the state he's in, he might just tell us."

"That's as maybe," countered Joe "but how do we find him?"

"Well, he couldn't possibly have driven anywhere," pondered Em. "Hang on! He lives in Devizes, right? So maybe he's walked back along the towpath!"

"Bit of a long shot isn't it?" asked Joe, doubtfully looking along the dark canal. "Must be miles."

"Oh, come on!" said Em pulling him by the arm, "we've got to catch him!"

The pair walked the first hundred metres or so warily, trying to make out all the black shapes and shadows cast across the narrow towpath. As their eyes began to adjust to the lower light, however, they became more confident and were able to keep up a steady pace.

At first, the sound of the boat engine springing into life further down the canal behind them didn't really register with them. As it's tone and it's volume rose, however, they hesitated momentarily and looked back.

Just around the last bend they had turned, a searchlight was now scanning across the canal.

"What are they looking for?" asked Joe, the answer becoming immediately apparent as a motorboat with the Policeman at the helm, appeared around the bend.

"Hemp ... or us!" whispered Em urgently. "Run!" and they sprinted for all they were worth.

The chill night air stung their lungs but the frosty mud path was solid underfoot. Hidden in the shadow of the path as it continued to curve round out of sight, they knew that they were never going to outpace a motorboat.

"Let's slide down the bank into the field," puffed Joe.

"Don't be stupid," puffed back Em. "The ones by All Cannings are five-metre drops into brambles. Keep going!"

They kept slogging along, their lungs wheezing, with frozen toes on leaden legs, the burbling sound of the motorboat ever present behind them.

"Up!" gasped Em, spotting a canal bridge looming up out of the blackness.

They scrambled, their feet slipping, up the steep rise and leapt full-length on the frozen earth behind the bridge's wall, just in time to avoid a sweep of the boat's searchlight. They lay motionless, covering the sound of their panting by burying their faces in their arms.

The boat chugged under the bridge and stopped.

"They couldn't have got further than this," said the voice of the Policeman. "Are you sure you saw them?"

"Yes sir!" replied another.

"Well, where the hell are they then?" said the Policeman.

"I don't know, sir," replied the second voice. "Could they have dropped down a ditch?"

"No, I don't think so," said the Policeman unimpressed. He paused. Em and Joe lay freezing and petrified, trying their hardest not to breathe.

"Come on," he added after what seemed like an eternity, "we've got bigger fish to fry." And then, as an afterthought, he added to no-one in particular: "You know, if I was those kids I'd mind my own business. They wouldn't want to end up like old Hemp now, would they?"

The boat's engine sprung back into life and the vessel gained speed and headed off towards Devizes.

***

As they shuffled back into the house, wet with cold sweat and covered in mud they met Dad, car keys in hand, in the hallway.

"What the hell's happened to you two?" he asked aghast.

"We thought we'd save you a trip and come back along the canal," said Em feebly.

"Did you swim?" asked Dad but he got no answer as the twins went off to shower and change.

***

Joe was woken by a sound he knew well. He tiptoed into Em's room and saw her sitting up in bed quietly weeping.

"More nightmares?" he asked, sitting next to her.

She nodded.

"Same one again?"

"Yes," she whispered.

"I'll sit with you," he said kindly.

After a while, Em lay down again and Joe curled up in Em's big, blue armchair. Em lay staring at the wall.

"What are you thinking about?" asked Joe. Em paused, weighing up her thoughts.

"I'm thinking about what Dad said about the truth being deadly," said Em.

"What about it?" said Joe.

"And then in all these nightmares there's always this rhyme "The road to truth is hard to tread but peace will soon be thine.'"

"So?"

"So it's mad but ... but what if Death is trying to lead us to the truth?"

***

An early morning stroll with her two basset hounds was one of the few real pleasures in life Mrs Bartlett still had. Long ago retired and having lost most of her family, her hearing and her sight, the joys of life were far less tangible than in her youth. But way before the traffic began to hum along Devizes' main arteries, she would enjoy the misty sunrise and a slow stroll alongside the town's famous run of locks up Caen Hill.

As the sun made a feeble effort to part the stiff, leaden winter clouds, she crunched along on the frosty grass verge in her stout, sensible shoes, her dogs panting and frisking to keep warm.

The early morning was a magical time for her and, depending on her mood, she would often transform her mundane surroundings into more fantastical objects. Park benches would become coffins and trees mushroom clouds. In happier moods, frost-covered grass would become sugar icing, traffic lights lollypops and zebra crossings stripy mint humbugs.

Not surprisingly, then, the police thought she was just another crank caller when she phoned them from a call box insisting she'd seen a giant gingerbread man floating in the water by the lock gates. Curious at her insistence, however, and given that it had been a quiet night, they decided to humour her and sent out a squad car.

"Well she was right about one thing, Sarge," the constable said, fishing the body out with a boat hook. "Face down in the water wearing all this brown corduroy he does look like a gingerbread man."

"Have a little respect, son," chided the Sergeant.

With the body safely on the side, the constable searched the body's clothing.

"I've got a wallet here, Sarge," said the constable, searching through it. "Good God!"

"What is it?" asked the Sergeant. The constable looked closer at the body's face.

"It's my old geography teacher!"

***

The Policeman's mobile rang at 2 a.m.

"What happened?" said the CMO abruptly.

"Hemp turned up at The Barge, got drunk and started mouthing off to those Priest kids so I liquidated him."

"And the kids?"

"They got away."

"GOT AWAY?!" screamed the CMO. "WHAT DO YOU MEAN "GOT AWAY"!"

"They've no idea what's going on, sir," said the Policeman, holding the phone away from his ear.

"Did they talk to Hemp?"

"Yes."

"Then kill them. Now!" the CMO ordered.

"Drowning an alcoholic depressive teacher is easy enough to pass off as a suicide. Killing two kids is something else."

"You almost managed it with your cornfield stunt," the CMO sneered. "Perhaps I should just ask you to keep tabs on them again and wait for their corpses to turn up."

"I was just trying to warn them off," the Policeman replied hotly.

"Yes, well it's a shame you didn't succeed. Look, I don't need to tell you things are at a delicate stage. One more security cock-up and we could all get it in the neck, literally. I want them under surveillance day and night. If they put a foot wrong, kill 'em."

CHAPTER 13
REMEMBRANCE

The snow came early that year, a sudden cold snap transforming the valley into a winter playground beyond the twins' wildest imagining. There were some snowboarders and the odd skier on the hillside. Even Mum got into the mood, arriving back from town on Saturday morning with a bright red plastic sled, and a vibrant pink snowsuit she'd seen in the window of Oxfam. She then proceeded to, literally, scream down the hillside all afternoon, leaving Em and Joe to cringe on the sidelines.

For one glorious, long weekend, it felt like they'd jetted away to the Alps, but it wasn't to last. A warmer wet front flowed in from the Atlantic and restored the damp, wet and miserable status quo just in time for Remembrance Day.

Joe was still smarting from the fact that his music teacher had not only nominated him to play *The Last Post* in school assembly (which rather incongruously doubled up as a memorial service for Mr Hemp) but also "asked" him to repeat the performance in the village church for the Sunday service as trumpet players were in short supply. Mum was thrilled and lost no time in telling Grandma, Grandpa and Aunt Mary, who were quick to dust off their cameras for the occasion. Em too was keen to offer her support. She hadn't been inside the church yet and wanted to know who in the village actually went there.

"And don't think you're not coming too," Anna said to Kim, when the twins were out of the room. "You may have deprived me of a church wedding and missed every Nativity play but you're coming to this."

"Actually, I'll be glad to go and I'm glad the kids are too," said Kim. "If there was ever a time when the folly of 'Onward Christian Soldiers' was most obvious, this is it. It's a lesson worth learning and I hope they profit by it."

***

The church was surprisingly small and dark inside, and its dozen or so pews were mostly occupied, much to Em's surprise. She remembered her first encounter with Mrs Ford in the street when taking J to the playground one afternoon, and remembered her quip that seeing as how they were Priests they would no doubt be spending a lot of time in church. How wrong could she have been!

Mum and Dad had varying views on religion and this, along with the fact that hardly any of their friends went to church, or perhaps just didn't admit that they did, meant the twins had no particular interest in going either. What idea they did have of Christian religion came from TV and involved as much about American evangelists in low budget TV movies as it did crusty old vicars from Agatha Christie's Miss Marple.

Em was surprised then, and a little pleased, when the vicar turned out to be a woman, and one who bore no resemblance whatsoever to Dawn French. She was equally surprised that her father not only knew when to stand, sit and kneel during the service but knew the tunes and most of the words to all the hymns too.

She almost fell out of her seat when the vicar called Kim forward to give a reading, and looking sideways she could see Mum was equally shocked. Kim addressed the congregation:

"This is a poem by the famous World War One poet, Wilfred Owen. It's called 'Dulce et decorum est'."

Em was shaken by what she heard. She'd never heard of the writer but his words were clearly those of a man suffering the true horrors of war. Moreover, the image of "drowning" in gas, was an all too strong reminder of Hemp's death and the fake policeman's threat.

She wasn't the only one shedding silent tears as Kim reached the final lines:

> "My friend, you would not tell with such
>   high zest
> To children ardent for some desperate
>   glory,
> The old Lie; Dulce et Decorum est
> Pro patria mori."

***

The service ended with the congregation filing out to the war memorial where wreaths of red poppies were laid and several old soldiers, including one in full regalia

127

with a sword and several lines of medals, saluted as Joe played *The Last Post*.

As they walked back along the road to home Mum put her arm through Dad's as he ruffled Joe's hair and said "Well done, son. That was great!"

"Never mind that," said Joe, "what about your reading? Rows of old biddies weeping! Mind you, that old duffer with the sword looked a bit stony-faced."

"It was beautiful," agreed Mum, "and so nice to have a pleasant surprise for a change."

"So what does it mean Dad?" asked Em, who had been lost in thought up to that point. "The last line of the poem."

"'It is sweet and fitting to die for one's country'."

"And is it?" said Joe.

"I'd much prefer it if you never had to find out," muttered Kim.

***

Em was quiet throughout Sunday lunch and everyone assumed she was still thinking about the service. In fact she had already moved on from it.

At the end of the meal, she went quietly to her room, leaving Joe to clear and help Mum wash up. When Joe finally caught up with her she was sitting silently in front of the computer.

"You all right?" he asked, putting a mug of coffee on the desk beside her.

"Yeah, thanks," she smiled. "I've been doing a lot of thinking." Joe looked at her quizzically.

"You haven't got religion, have you?" he grinned.

"No, but I do think I've 'seen the light'."

"Come again?"

"The poem that Dad read," Em explained. "'It is good to die for your country', or whatever." Joe's face remained blank. "Do you remember when we went into town on our own the first time, after our boots were stolen?"

"And we'd met that hippy on the boat?" asked Joe.

"Yes, that time," agreed Em. "We went into the library and I was looking up the historic sites and you asked me if I'd heard of Porton Down."

"Uh huh."

"And you told me that there was some scandal about them testing stuff on unsuspecting soldiers."

"Yeah."

"Well I've looked it up and I think I've discovered something interesting."

***

The twins talked for over an hour while overhead J took his afternoon nap and Mum and Dad gave the weak afternoon film the only reception it deserved, a barrage of stereo snoring from either end of the sitting room sofa.

The twins were still talking.

"Yes," said Em, "and it turns out the place was actually set up during the First World War to research the use of poison gas, just like the stuff used in the poem Dad read this morning."

"OK," said Joe. "So let's just assume it's possible you've hit on something here. What chance have we got of finding someone we can trust who really knows what the army gets up to around here and would actually talk to us about it? We don't want to end up like Hemp. I don't care what they say, I don't think he just slipped into the water and drowned." Em thought for a moment.

"I know Gran said we shouldn't bother him, but what about General Harris?" said Em. "He hasn't been retired that long and Grandpa said he knew the Plain well and even thought he had links to Porton Down."

"I dunno," said Joe doubtfully. "Gran said he was pretty upset about losing his wife. She didn't exactly say it but I got the impression that she thinks he's gone a bit, you know, ... odd."

"Oh, come on! That was last year! We've got to find out!" said Em. And then she pressed home her advantage: "And just imagine the look on Jordan's face if I'm right!"

A glimmer of a smile raised the corners of Joe's mouth. "Well, all right, but you can do the talking."

"Don't I always?" shrugged Em.

***

You didn't need to be a genius to work out what sort of person lived in The Bastion. The front gates reminded the twins of some they'd seen on Horseguard's Parade on a school trip to Central London, and they even had a pair of ornamental sentry boxes either side.

The drive ran straight through the centre of ranks of spiky garden shrubs, like waves of heavily armed infantrymen guarding a khaki-coloured building entrenched behind the final line of defence, a two metre high holly hedge. The front door, flanked by two enormous artillery shells, was solid oak peppered with black, iron bolts.

They had crunched up the frosty, gravel drive in silence. "Are you really sure about this?" half whispered Joe, his breath billowing white clouds into the chilly air. The sun was just going down and what had been a cold, clear winter's day was quickly becoming a freezing, dark winter's night.

"No, but I just feel we're so close," replied Em, her hand hovering near the bell push.

With a crack like a rifle shot the door swung open.

A red-faced, white-haired man, at least two metres tall, stared down a long, straight nose at them.

"Yes?" he boomed and the twins took a step back and stood up straight. For a moment they were stunned, staring at this giant, an expanse of green tweed topped off with an enormous, snowy moustache.

"Oh, er, hello, er, sir, we're, er, collecting for the poor," Joe blurted out in total panic.

"What? Don't talk utter rot, man. There aren't any poor people around here," blasted the General with a steely glint in his eye. Em looked down at his arms to make sure he wasn't cradling a shotgun.

"I'm sorry," said Em. "We're Bob King's grandchildren. We wanted to meet you."

"Oh, really?" said the General suspiciously.

"Yes, we're doing a school project about the army on Salisbury Plain and we understand you would know more than anyone else around here."

"Humphh!" grunted the old soldier. "Well, that sounds more likely." He hesitated a moment and then stood aside. "Well, I suppose you'd better come in."

***

Em's first impression was that the house was more like a gallery than a home. Spotlessly clean with hard wood parquet flooring and row upon row of portraits of military types, some face on, some in profile and rather a lot sitting bolt upright on sleekly groomed horses. There weren't any of what you might call personal effects, just orderly displays of medals, badges and military books in glass cases. A woman's touch, as Mum would say, was clearly lacking.

The twins followed the direction of the General's outstretched arm into the drawing room.

"Sit!" snapped the General, indicating a small, green leather sofa facing a matching wing-backed armchair with a Persian rug between them, all aligned at a perfect right angle to the fireplace.

The twins hesitated for a moment, making sure this order was directed at them and not some poor dog, but as one failed to materialise, they promptly obeyed, wedging themselves shoulder to shoulder on the too-small sofa.

Joe felt a sudden twinge of uneasiness as he remembered what Mr Hemp had said about tall men barking orders at him.

"Bob King's grandchildren, eh?" said the General, half to himself. "And what do you want to know from me?" He sat in his wing-backed chair.

"Well sir," said Joe, trying to redeem himself. "We've only recently moved to the area and we're interested in the crop circles."

"That rubbish," snorted the General. "What's that got to do with the army?"

132

"Well, nothing," admitted Em, "but, well, we were wondering what you could tell us about Porton Down."

"Porton Down?" repeated the General slowly.

Em suddenly wished she'd given more thought to how to approach this meeting. She hurriedly tried again. "You see, we, well, we were told you knew all about that too and we have this theory that the crop circles and the experiments are linked in some way."

"Oh really." It was more a statement than a question.

"Yes," hurried on Em, glad to feel she had got the man's attention. "We've been thinking about all the military activity in the area, the firing on Salisbury Plain, all the aircraft flying around the place, and then the crop circles appearing in the fields. You see, it seems to us that if the army came under pressure not to experiment on its own troops any more or came to the limit of what they could do in a laboratory, they might be tempted to try things out in the wider world. And where better than a valley enclosed by high hills just north of Salisbury Plain where there was every reason to have aircraft flying over? That way they could drop whatever they were testing and no-one would suspect."

Joe took up the story:

"So they set up all the local doctors and hospitals, without them even knowing it, to log the effects or, perhaps, the spread of a more harmless version of a virus or bacterium that closely resembles a much deadlier version that would be used against an enemy."

"The only problem was though," continued Em, "that every now and then the release of the stuff from the planes would go wrong and leave suspicious marks on the crops in the valley. It could have totally ruined the experiment if the stuff had got into the food supply and was spread across the country or even further and then been detected somehow. So the only thing to do was to decontaminate the crops without the farmers realising it. And that's where the crop circles come in.

"The method they were using flattened and slightly irradiated the crops or left a detectable electrical field. The marks left behind were so noticeable that a cover story was needed. So they latched onto the UFO myth used so successfully by the Americans to explain away sightings of their top secret spy and space projects. They flattened the crops out in the classic 'flying saucer' shape and if any samples were needed, they used a laser to give the impression of some alien technology at work."

"Obviously," Joe went on, "news of the circles was going to spread so the usual groups of hippies, whackos and gullible idiots were encouraged to believe in the alien theory, while drunk students and the like were equally encouraged to go out with some rope, barrels and planks of wood and make their own. And if anyone got too close to the truth, they were quickly warned off."

"So," added Em, relieved and with an air of triumph, "we were wondering whether you could tell us anything?"

There was a long pause, interrupted only by the crackling of logs burning in the grate.

"No," said the General finally in a strong, level voice "I could not. But perhaps I would be permitted to ask *you* a question?"

"Er, of course," stuttered Em, unnerved by his aggressive politeness.

"Does anyone know you came here?" he said through gritted teeth.

"What?" Em's voice quivered.

"Did you tell anyone you were coming here?" repeated the General, growling now.

"Of course we did," said Joe, too quickly to be convincing.

"You're liars, both of you!" hissed the General, suddenly stepping forward onto the rug and grasping a long, iron poker from beside the fireplace. "You come in here with your half-baked theories about the army, MY army," Joe and Em were too terrified to dodge his spittle, "poisoning people. And what if we were, eh? WHAT IF WE WERE?"

"Your generation hasn't got a clue. Spawned by a bunch of filthy, long-haired hippies who spent the sixties smoking dope and having 'love children' all over the place, whilst yours truly was making the world a safer place for them. What fools we were! We thought we were fighting the communists but it turns out that the bleeding heart socialists were already in our midst. And what do I get for my hard work? NOTHING! No respect, no recognition, I can't even hunt a bloody fox without some damn fool policeman knocking on my door.

"So, so what? So what if we had to test our weapons out? Open an animal testing laboratory and thousands of protesters turn out. Ask them if they'd like to make the world a better place by taking the lab rat's place and you won't get much of a queue, let me tell you!

"What you people don't understand is that for us to be strong, people have to die. Some have to die to give us their land and some have to die to give us their oil but most of all they have to die because they're in the wrong place at the wrong time." and he lowered his voice to a guttural growl. "Just like you."

Without warning he swung the poker full circle landing it with a resounding "Whump!" The twins reacted just in time to allow the poker a few millimetres space between them as they dived to the floor in opposite directions, in what would have looked to any outside observer like some sort of miraculous separation of Siamese twins.

Swearing at his failure to make contact, the General had already managed to raise his improvised weapon again and was preparing to bring it down on Em who was cowering, petrified beside the sofa. But just as his twisted smile registered his deadly intent he felt his feet begin to slip from under him. Em looked up to see the General falling, rigid to the last, like a mighty redwood tree, in what seemed like slow motion. The poker clanged to the floor as his head cracked open on the sharp corner of the fireplace, splattering blood across the flecked granite.

As Em slowly looked back across the floor, she saw Joe, crouching, holding the edge of the rug in his hands, his eyes wide and his mouth open in silent horror.

Without a word she leapt up, dragged Joe to his feet, and they ran from the house, Em slamming the door behind them.

***

It was dark now and the icy air stung their lungs as they sprinted along the lane towards home.

"Slow down!" wheezed Em, grabbing Joe's arm. "We've got to slow down! Walk!"

Joe slackened his pace under the influence of Em's firm grip.

They walked in an uneasy silence until they reached the stable yard.

"We've got to tell someone," whispered Joe urgently.

"No, we've got to act normally. No-one knows we were there. What are we going to say? 'He attacked us so we killed him?'"

"It was an accident," Joe pleaded, "I was trying to save you!"

"Yes ... yes, you did. Thank you," and she hugged him. Their minds were still so full of their escape that there was none of the usual sense of awkwardness.

"Nice to see you two getting on so well," shouted Dad, who had opened the kitchen window. "Come in and wash your hands. I've made pizza!"

CHAPTER 14
THE TOMB OF THE WELL-KNOWN SOLDIER

A tense and restless night followed a similar evening with Em and Joe sitting in their separate bedrooms.

Breakfast the next morning was disturbed by an unfamiliar sight.

"Isn't that a police car that's just gone past?" said Mum, who was standing at the kitchen sink. Dad looked up from his paper and in her direction, just in time to miss the worried glance Joe had shot at Em. Em's wide-eyed firm stare told Joe to hold his tongue.

"It's going up to The Bastion," continued Mum. "It's probably a break-in. There's a mini crime wave going on at the moment. Did you get to the report in the paper yet?"

"No, but I shouldn't worry," said Dad returning his attention to the pages spread across the table. "Anyone breaking in here to steal Christmas presents will be sorely disappointed."

***

As in any small community, news of the General's demise spread rapidly. Mrs Potts, the cleaner, had found him. Letting herself in at 7 a.m. sharp (the General, she told the police, was very particular about such things), she was surprised to see that the curtains were still drawn in the General's office and had gone to investigate. Getting no reply to her calls, her search led her to the drawing room and a grisly discovery.

"He was firm but fair," she had sobbed to a comforting policewoman. "Always had to have things just so, but he was always generous at Christmas. Fifty pounds he gave me last year. Fifty pounds! There's not many like that round here, I can tell you.

"I warned him about that hearthrug. I said to him, I said 'It's lethal' I said. A rug like that on a polished floor but he wouldn't have it. I tried popping the edge of it under the feet of the sofa but he'd just pull it out again as soon as I'd gone."

Mrs Potts gave the police details of the General's only living relative, a sister in Worthing. The arrangements were made for a rather grand funeral on what turned out to be a very chilly December day.

***

"But why do *we* have to go?" Joe asked Mum for the umpteenth time.

"It's a small village," insisted Mum. "Everyone's going. And besides, Grandma and Grandpa knew him and so did I a long time ago, so we're doubly obliged to go. If we want to be accepted here, we need to join in and that means not just the nice things like summer fetes."

The weeks had passed quickly and the sheer normality of everyday life had overshadowed the twins' horrific secret. They never spoke of it and as a result spoke less and less together. But this was not all that had changed. Despite the intense anxiety of her every waking moment, Em's nights were now tranquil and uninterrupted; miraculously, the nightmares had ceased.

The twins were horrified to learn that not only did Mum insist they went to the funeral but she had volunteered them to hand round drinks and sandwiches at the wake.

The funeral passed off without incident, Em's silent tears covered by the loud sniffing and nose-blowing of Mrs Potts several rows in front of her.

As the service ended and the pews emptied Em hung back and whispered desperately to Joe: "I can't go through with this! I can't go back in that house!"

"We'll get through it," said Joe with a strong, assuring voice she'd never heard before. "We have to."

The walk up the street towards The Bastion was the longest of their lives, the rhythm of their steps accompanying the pounding of their hearts.

"Look!" suddenly shouted Em grasping Joe's arm, and raising a few tuts from fellow mourners in the process. She lowered her voice: "They're all going into the village hall!"

"Yes, didn't I tell you?" said Mum quizzically.

"No ... no you didn't," said Joe as levelly as possible, and removing Em's vice-like grip from his forearm as subtly as he could.

***

Bizarrely enough, the wake was quite a jolly affair. There was a fair amount of spirits on offer and the general hubbub was soon punctuated by the odd snort of laughter. Circulating amongst the various little huddles of mourners with trays of drinks and nibbles, Em and Joe picked up odd snippets of conversation.

"He was the last of dying breed"..."since Marjorie's death he was a changed man" ..."it was a merciful release, really" ..."no way for an old soldier to go"..."coppers say he slipped poking the fire!"... "I told him about that hearthrug a thousand times!"

After an hour, Dad popped his head into the little kitchen and told Em and Joe he thought they'd shown willing and done their bit and could all go home now.

***

Em and Joe spent a miserable afternoon sitting in the dining room pretending to be doing their homework. Neither of them spoke. The atmosphere was deadly.

Eventually, after two hours of total silence, Joe spoke in the same strong tone he had used in church that morning: "We've got to tell someone what we did, Em." Em heaved a deep sigh.

"What did we do, Joe? Some old madman tried to kill *us*." She paused and looked him straight in the eye. "No-one can ever know about this. It wasn't our fault."

"What wasn't your fault?" said Dad popping his head around the door. "And don't accuse me of eavesdropping, I was coming to tell you dinner's ready. Come on. Whose cat have you poisoned now?"

"It's not funny, Dad" said Joe. "We've really done something … terrible."

Dad looked into their eyes and saw something new. "OK, look, your Mum's a bit low after the funeral, so let's get through dinner, set her up with a costume drama and a box of chocolates and then we can discuss this. If she asks, I'm helping you with your school project." The twins swapped a pained look. "What, is that too lame an excuse?"

"No, Dad, it's fine," sighed Em.

***

"OK," said Dad. "I'm all ears."

He sat, a coffee mug cradled in his hands, leaning back in the green leather office chair he thought made him look like the CEO of a big corporation. The fact that it normally resided underneath his makeshift desk of an old door on two wooden trestles, when it wasn't, as now, pulled up to the kitchen table, failed to shatter the illusion for him. But then neither did the fact that he was wearing fluffy reindeer slippers.

Em and Joe, sat nervously at the other side of the table, said nothing.

"OK, let me put that another way: What have you stolen?"

"A life?" whispered Em, looking down into her lap.

"Wha … Damn!" Losing his balance, Dad's chair sprung forward making him spill some of his coffee in his lap. He jumped up and grabbed a teacloth to mop up the worst and then with a flash of realisation turned towards them. "Good God! You don't mean you had anything to do with the death of that old …"

"It wasn't our fault," gulped Em, welling up with emotion. "He tried to kill us!'

"All right, all right," soothed Dad, sitting down again and taking Em's hand. "Keep your voice down, we need to stay calm." He paused. "Joe, can you tell me what happened?"

"It was me," said Joe, suddenly looking up and meeting his Dad's concerned gaze as the truth he had tried so hard to conceal spilled out. "He was going to bash Em's head in with a poker so I tried to make him miss by pulling at the rug but it just flew out from under him and he fell ..." His words evaporated as he remembered the crack of the General's head hitting the hearth and the splattering of blood.

"But why were you even there?" Dad continued.

"Our school project," whispered Em. "We wanted to find a logical reason for the crop circles. We came up with a theory, we just sort of made it up, but we thought ... oh, I don't know exactly what we thought ... but maybe he'd tell us something or say something interesting."

"But what did you say to him to make him react like that?" asked Dad.

"We told him we thought the crop circles were evidence of the army covering up a mass experiment of chemical and biological weapons on the local people," said Em. She explained the whole theory while Dad sat in stunned silence.

Dad whistled. "You don't pull any punches, do you? So what did he say?"

"He just sort of ranted on at us about communists, fox-hunting and love children or something and then attacked us with a poker," said Em flatly. "But I still can't see why?"

"Can't you?" sighed Dad. "From what I've heard of him he was a soldier of the old school; Queen and Country above all else. He's sitting up there in his fortress of a house, festering in his traditions and with a mindset of 'whatever happens today is never as good as it was in my day'. All he can see in the world is doom and decay. Children who talk back, muggers, murderers and worse. And who's to say that sometimes he may not have had a point?

"You walked in there with a story that would taint his precious army and he saw red. Who knows, you may have stumbled on the truth, or got near it, but I really don't think it would have mattered to him either way."

"So he tried to kill us to save the army's reputation?" asked Em.

"People have died for much less," sighed Kim, running his hand across his face.

There was another pause. Dad leant back in his chair.

"So what happened to 'don't mess with things you don't understand'?" he sighed.

"You also told us to look for the truth," muttered Joe.

"Yes, and I also said that the truth is a very dangerous thing to set out before those who don't want to accept it," Dad snapped. "They create their own reality, only believing what they want to believe in, because it makes them feel safe."

"Look! None of that matters any more," pleaded Em. "What are we going to do?"

Dad thought for a moment. The ticking of the kitchen clock filling the silence.

"We're not going to do anything," said Dad simply. "The police, the general's family and the people of the village have their truth and they're happy with it. He was an objectionable, slightly senile and, we now know, very dangerous old man. Whether he was involved in all the horrific stuff at Porton Down or not, we don't know, but he tried to kill you so there is no reason to feel guilty about an accident that took place when you were trying to defend yourselves."

"But I killed him," Joe almost whispered.

"No, Joe," said Dad, "you saved Em's life and I'm proud of you and very grateful."

They sat in silence, the faint sound of Mum's television programme in the background.

"So what happens now?" sniffed Em.

"Nothing," said Dad. "And I mean nothing. No word of this to anyone, no more questions and no more project. Just cobble together the usual inconclusive stuff about freak weather patterns and leave it at that."

"You mean, that's it? Just forget it?" said Joe.

"Sometimes it's better to forget what you know and move on," insisted Dad. "It's safer and you live a much happier life."

"But what if it's still going on?" said Em. "The experiments, I mean. Shouldn't we go away from here?"

"Look, I'm not saying I believe your theory for one minute," said Dad. "I just think you were attacked by a mad old man, but let's assume just for a moment that you may have been right.

"Back in the 70s and 80s this place was a complete backwater so, yes, it's possible something went on, but not now. The place is crawling with tourists, croppies and archaeologists looking for leylines, rocks and evidence of little green men. This is probably one of the most photographed and analysed areas in the world.

"If they wanted to carry on doing this sort of stuff, they'd do it somewhere where the outside world has no access, like one of those sand boxes they keep invading in the Middle East. Sadly, no-one's going to bat an eyelid at a few extra deaths out there."

"So we're staying here then?" said Em, dejectedly.

"Em," smiled Dad, "life is all about taking calculated risks. Something may have happened here a long time ago but it's highly unlikely it's still happening now. It's a good, clean and safe place to live. We have to balance that against the fact that if we go back to the city, we're all going to get poisoned by the fumes, and I'll be the first one to go."

"But I miss the city."

"So do I, in some ways," said Dad, "but we're all making new friends, our old ones are always welcome to come and stay and we can always go and see them. I promise."

"So we're not going back, then?" Em all but whispered.

"Do you really want to go?" Dad asked softly.

There was a long pause.

"Don't wanna go!" wailed J, who'd silently wandered into the room unnoticed in his Thomas the Tank Engine pyjamas.

"I know, I know," said Em soothingly, rushing to pick him up, "and we don't have to. This is our home now and we don't have to move ever again."

***

The Policeman and the Chief Medical Officer sat side by side in the Hercules transport plane as it prepared for take-off.

"You appreciate that if you disobey any of my orders out there, they'll never find your body," muttered the CMO in a threatening tone.

"Yessir!"

"We could always shake on it," said the CMO with a twisted smile.

"That won't be necessary, sir."

"Good! I won't jeopardise a whole operation because some fool doesn't want some kids' blood on his hands."

"No sir."

"I know what you were thinking: The programme was coming to a close and they'd no idea what they'd stumbled into. Lucky for you the General scared the hell out of them!"

"Yessir!"

"Sort of poetic him dying at their hands though," the CMO added wistfully, turning to take a last look out of the window at British soil. "The old bastard had more blood on his hands than all the rest of us put together."

After a pause the CMO added, "Anyway, if you were wondering about what's going to happen to them, I shouldn't worry. I sent them a little leaving present."

CHAPTER 15
THE GIFT OF PEACE?

The run up to Christmas was one of the happiest Em could remember. Tom wrote her an actual letter saying he had persuaded his parents to spend Christmas in the UK this year so they could meet up. Joe was busy trying to find his mysterious redhead again (he still hadn't got her phone number) and Dad had found a proper full-time job on the local paper.

Day after day, the postman brought a new handful of Christmas cards to decorate the house with, and day after day, Em would indulge one of her favourite pleasures and rush down to grab them off the mat first.

And so two days before Christmas, as she gathered up the post, she was instantly drawn out of curiosity to the small red envelope with the printed label bearing her and Joe's full names. Ripping it open, she smiled quizzically at the odd little card with an angel motif and "The Gift of Eternal Peace" printed on the front.

As she opened it, a waft of something chemical provoked an instinctive sense of foreboding. The first line of the neat handwritten message froze her to the spot:

"We know what you did."

Panic rising within her, Em read on.

"Forget all you know and Peace will be yours forever."

As she stared at the words they began to fade until, after just a few short seconds, they had disappeared entirely.

Em stood stunned, trying to take this in. Eventually, Joe wandered into the hallway to find her still staring at the blank card.

"What's it mean?" he asked.

Em started to smile. "It means it's all over. Forever." She hugged him. "Merry Christmas Joe!"

***

Christmas Eve was all it should ever be. Anna volunteered Baby J to play a lamb in the toddler group's nativity play. Carol singers came round to slurp mulled wine and devour mince pies, and the little church's bells rang out across the Vale. A scattering of snow fell from a mainly clear sky and Mars continued to sparkle brightly in the east.

Mum and Dad had wanted to take all the family to the pub for dinner but they could only get a table for two. Tired out after all the excitement and having gone down with colds the day before, Em and Joe had happily volunteered to babysit, Dad slipping them a few notes for the takeaway of their choice.

Just after midnight, as Joe and Em were dozing in front of a warm TV and cold pizza box, waiting for Mum and Dad to come home, there was a shuffling of feet outside the front door followed by a tuneless chorus of "We Three Kings of Orient Are".

"Bit late for carol singers," yawned Joe, stretching and going to open up.

"It's the Grands with Great Aunt Mary on their way back from Midnight Mass," said Em, peeping round the edge of the curtain. "The Three Kings, get it?!" Joe groaned and opened the door to see them standing in the newly fallen snow with armfuls of presents.

"Hello you two!" boomed Grandpa, who wasn't beyond slipping a hip flask of brandy into his pocket on such occasions. He rushed in, throwing down his presents and giving the twins a joint bear hug. "My little Mary and Joseph left holding the baby because there's no room at the inn!"

"Bob," sighed Grandma, putting a hand on his sleeve.

"Yes, dear?"

"Be quiet, darling. You'll wake the baby."

"Yes, dear."